infinity plus

MICROCOSMS

TONY**BALLANTYNE**
ERIC**BROWN**

MICRO...

TWENTY-ONE STORIES BY
TONY BALLANTYNE

...COSMS

TWENTY-ONE STORIES BY
ERIC BROWN

INTRODUCTION TO *MICRO...*

THIS VOLUME CAME ABOUT ONE summer a few years ago when Tony came up to Scotland with his family. We were wandering around the pretty seaside town of North Berwick and talking about recent short stories we'd written. Tony happened to mention that he was working on some short-shorts, which he hoped to place with *Nature*, and I mentioned a short-short market that I'd recently sold to, *Daily SF*. I then suggested that, when we had enough tales to form a volume, we should gather them all together and attempt to find a publisher.

Years passed; we wrote short-shorts between bigger projects, and Keith Brooke who runs Infinity Plus Books expressed an interest in publishing *Microcosms*.

Tony Ballantyne is not only a fine novelist – as equally gifted in the Hard SF sub-genre as in Fantasy – but he's a skilled short-story writer, with several of his stories gracing the pages of *Analog* and other top markets, and appearing in Best of the Year anthologies. He also excels at the short-short story, where originality and incisive vision are requisite. In his intelligence, playful wit and economy of language, the writer he most reminds me of is the late, great Robert Sheckley. This volume contains such gems as "Dear Burglar", "The Cleverest Man in the World", and "The Scooped Out Man" – the latter an alien invasion tale to end them all. But my favourite is the irreverent, witty, self-referential story about a writer, "Another (almost) True Story", a tale which I would have given my right arm to have written.

And now, for fear of this introduction becoming longer than some of the short-shorts herein, I'll sign off.

Eric Brown
Cockburnspath
2016

INTRODUCTION TO ... COSMS

ERIC AND I MET AT the 2Kon SF convention in Glasgow in the year 2000. We both had a short story up for the BSFA award. Eric won, I lost, but by way of consolation I made a great friend.

Friendship aside, I remain a massive fan of Eric's. He has written an impressive number of novels and short stories; his output includes what is possibly my favourite short story collection ever: *Kethani* (Solaris 2008). As well as being a prolific writer he is an eminent critic with a deep knowledge of the genre. He is a keen champion of the new, the forgotten and the underrated, and is a valuable source of advice to writers no matter where they are in their career (he taught me the trick of just listening to the subconscious, of getting things down as quickly as possible on the page).

In this collection you'll find scintillating flashes of his talent. His writing is by turns witty, melancholic, horrifying and deceptively gentle, but always imbued with his trademark sense of humanity. Take a look at "In the Recovery Room", "Meeting Myself on Planet Earth", "Memorial" and "The History of Earth" to see what I mean.

What the heck. Read them all, they're all good. He deserved that award. And the other ones…

Tony Ballantyne
Oldham
2016

THE ROBOT AND THE OCTOPUS

TONY BALLANTYNE

"SIT DOWN AND SHUT UP!"

Kevin did as he was told. He was in enough trouble already.

"We just had this couriered over from the coast," said Gabi, sliding the oversized cassette into the machine. She dimmed the lights and then perched her elegant bottom on the edge of the table, just by the Colonel. Fuzzy tones danced across the TV screen.

"Security camera from another computer store," explained Gabi, lighting a cigarette. "Here it comes…"

The door to the store exploded inwards and the robot strode into view.

"Look, I told you, this is nothing to do with me!" Kevin twisted frantically in his chair.

"You were told to shut up," snapped the Colonel.

On the screen, the robot moved through the shop, pulling behind it the trolley that carried the octopus's tank. The octopus was lit up like a falling firework in fiery red and yellow, its strange rectangular eyes watching the panic in the store as the robot walked from shelf to shelf, pulling down blister packs and scanning their contents.

"Why the hell does it drag that octopus everywhere?" shouted the Colonel, in frustration.

"I told you, I don't know!" Kevin's voice was shrill with panic. "This has nothing to do with me."

"Typical engineer. Never takes the blame." The Colonel turned back to the screen to look at the group of customers huddled in the corner of the room. "Why don't they run?" he complained. "They're right by the door!"

Gabi took the cigarette from her mouth and held it in her perfect white fingers, red nail polish shining like blood.

"We think the robot is emitting some sort of subsonic growl that disturbs the nervous system. It stole a sound system from a store in Brighton."

"It's ridiculous, how can things go so badly wrong?" The Colonel clenched his fists in frustration.

"With respect, Colonel," said Gabi in tones that implied no respect at all, "things are working exactly as they should. The nanotechs are designed to protect themselves. They've been redesigning that robot's body to do exactly that. It's working too. We can't stop it."

"It's working too," mimicked the Colonel, sarcastically. "So how do you explain the octopus? How do you explain that?" He pointed to the screen just as the robot, having obviously found the parts needed, pulled one of the cowering customers from the crowd and chopped her up with a large sword. It threw the pieces into the tank. The robot headed back out into the street, dragging the feasting octopus behind it.

"Well?" asked the Colonel. He glared at Kevin again. "Well?"

"I don't know," said Kevin "Maybe the robot just likes octopuses."

"Octopi," said Gabi. She gazed at the young man. "Kevin, you must have some idea. Where will the robot strike next?"

Kevin held up his hands in despair.

"I don't know. That's the point. I built those nanotechs to think for themselves! Individually they can do little more than add up or make logical comparisons, but they are designed to link up to form a neural net. They're like a mobile brain. A brain that can possess objects! That's what your company paid me to build." He stabbed an accusing finger at Gabi.

"We didn't pay you to allow them to escape," she replied coolly. "You let them get into that robot."

"Me?" said Kevin. "I've never seen that robot in my life. It certainly wasn't anywhere in my part of the research centre!" He gazed accusingly at Gabi. "What else was your company doing, Gabi? All that secrecy. All those mysterious rooms. What am I being made the scapegoat for?"

The Colonel shook his head.

"Son, part of growing up is knowing when to accept responsibility for your mistakes…"

"Gentlemen," said Gabi in brittle tones. She took another pull on her cigarette, blew out a cloud of smoke. "We need to focus on what's important here. We have millions of dollars worth of nanotechs walking round in a robot, dragging an octopus behind them."

"Maybe if we took a moment to think about this. Maybe it's not what it looks like…"

"We haven't got a moment, son! That robot of yours has been walking around Europe, stealing parts to make itself stronger! Anyone who gets in its way gets fed to the octopus! Why?"

"I told you! It's not my robot…"

There was a brief tap on the door. A face appeared.

"Sir, turn to channel nine, immediately!"

Gabi stopped the tape and flicked the channels on the TV. The man at the door was breathless with excitement.

"We've caught it! Picked it up with a giant magnet slung beneath a helicopter!"

"Good work, Evans!"

The TV screen showed the robot being carried away by the helicopter. It waved a mournful goodbye to the octopus, watching from the tank.

Gabi stood up and smoothed the creases from her expensive suit.

"Come on, Colonel," she said. "Damage limitation." The two of them headed out of the room. Gabi paused for a moment in the doorway, looking at Kevin.

"We'll deal with you later."

"But I didn't do…"

Kevin lapsed into silence. They weren't listening to him. That was the trouble with the non-scientifically minded. They just accepted everything at face value. They didn't stop to consider the wider picture. Now they had caught the robot, they had lost interest in the octopus.

It had to be important. Why would a robot want an octopus? For a pet? He looked at the screen and saw his answer.

The octopus was climbing from the tank. It seemed to be looking for something.

So that's where the nanotechs went, thought Kevin. No wonder it's so hungry for flesh. The nanotechs will need lots of energy.

Flopping its way down the side of the tank, the octopus went looking for materials to build itself another robot.

DIFFERENCES

ERIC BROWN

THIS MUCH I ACCEPT: I am guilty. I do not dispute the charge. I do, however, contest the nature of the crime with which I am charged.

I sat in the waiting room and watched, through the gallery window, the flow of humanity pass by on their way to the manufactories. They all wore the white two-piece uniform identical to my own and moved with a sense of purpose which struck me as mechanical.

I suspected these thoughts were heretical, but I was past caring.

There was no-one else in the waiting room outside office 30 of the Department for Social Correction. I wondered how long I would be made to wait.

Perhaps thirty minutes later a door slid open in the white wall before me, and a voice spoke. "Daniels 347. Enter."

I stood and entered the room.

A citizen sat behind a white, empty desk.

Se regarded me impassively. A camera watched me from the ceiling.

"I am Arkinen 88," se said. "Be seated."

I sat down. I was determined to betray no emotion.

I noticed, on the desk before Arkinen 88, the offending object.

Se said, "On the 34th of Fourth Month, 3055, you were found in possession of... this." Arkinen 88 tapped the object, which was wrapped in clear plastic as if to contain an infection. "Do you deny the charge, Daniels 347?"

"I do not."

"I will therefore request that you answer the following questions truthfully. Your cooperation in this matter might lead to the mitigation of your punishment."

I inclined my head, but I knew se was lying. I knew full well what my punishment would be.

Se said, "Now, who gave you this, Daniels 347?"

"No-one gave me it. I found it."

"Where did you find it?"

"In refectory 75, level 34."

"That is a lie. Monitors show no record of this object being in situ in refectory 75." Se paused. "Where did you find it, Daniels 347?"

"In refectory 75, level 34."

"That is a lie. If you persist in lying, you will receive the ultimate punishment."

I was calm. I stared back, mirroring Arkinen 88's impassive expression.

Se went on, "Who gave it to you, Daniels 347?"

"No-one gave it to me."

Se sighed. "You are not helping yourself, Daniels 347. Do you not wish to live?"

I told myself that I was ready for death. I said nothing.

Se said, "You will go to office 45 of the Department for Social Correction at 1400 hours. There, the duty officer will decide upon your punishment. Dismissed."

I stood and walked from the room without a glance at Arkinen 88.

ON THE WAY TO OFFICE 45 of the Department for Social Correction, I decided to stop by the sexorium for the very last time.

I took my place in line with the other citizens and in due course arrived at the cubicle. I entered and locked the door behind me. I lowered my shorts and allowed my genitalia to be manipulated by the extrusion that emerged from the wall. I sighed and gripped the hand-holds, placed my forehead against the padded bar and stared into the screen. A fractal pattern played, with a soothing musical accompaniment. Ecstasy ensued. Duly I orgasmed.

I withdrew from the extrusion, pulled up my shorts and left the cubicle.

The time was 1300.

I SAT ON A CHAIR in the empty waiting room and stared at the door to office 45. I thought of what Rodriguez 89 had passed on to me. Se had suggested that, to attain the full benefit from the object – the book, se had called it – I should abstain from taking my daily dosage of pharmaceuticals dispensed by my cell.

I had duly abstained, then read the book.

Now I thought of the scenes from the book, and the many differences between the world portrayed, and our world.

The citizens of that world had lived *outside*. The author had described the sensation of sunlight and wind and rain upon the flesh. Although I understood the concept of these terms, I could not imagine the physical reality of experiencing these sensations.

The lack of drugs in my system, said Rodriguez 89, would allow me for the first time in my life to see *this* world for what it was.

The authorities claim that we live in a wondrous modern age, the best of all possible times, but I had read of a time when citizens were free, when citizens could travel the world, take up whatever professions they wished…

When citizens could eat whatever they wished…

When citizens could speak to whoever they chose…

When citizens could love other citizens…

And now, because the drug was no longer in my system, I could weep.

THE DOOR TO OFFICE 45 opened and a voice called, "Daniels 347. Enter."

I stood and entered the room.

An officer sat behind a desk. Se gestured for me to sit down.

"Daniels 347, I am Richter 995. I represent the highest level of the Corrective Judiciary. I am here to ask you certain questions. Truthful answers will elicit appropriate leniency in the matter of your punishment."

Se stared at me, impassive.

"Now, who gave you the book?"

"I found the book in refectory 75, level 34."

Richter 995 made no facial expression.

Se said, "Do you realise why you are being prosecuted, Daniels 347?"

I nodded. "I possessed a banned object."

"And the reason the object is banned?"

"Because it tells of a time when the world was... different."

"Not only that," said Richter 995, "it promotes the heretical idea that difference is acceptable in a just and equitable society. This is erroneous thinking. Do you see the error of its ideas?"

I shook my head. "It showed a world where difference was to be celebrated," I said. "It told of..." I took a breath, my heart hammering with the knowledge of my heresy, "it told of *men* and *women*, of how they came together and *made love...*" The words felt like molten lead on my tongue.

"Enough!" Richter 995 said. "I have heard enough. You will be found guilty, and your punishment communicated to you in due course. Dismissed."

I stood and left the room, my thoughts full of a world other than this one.

I RETURNED TO MY CELL and sat on the bed, staring at the screen on the wall.

One hour later the screen chimed and my sentence appeared on its surface. "Daniels 347," I read, "you have been found guilty of breaking code 675b, clause xi. You are duly ordered to proceed to euthanarium 12 on level 45, before 1800 hours of this day. In accordance with the law of the land, you have the right to record your reaction to the sentence. This does not constitute an appeal. It is merely a citizen's right to state subjective fact."

I stared at the screen and smiled.

I considered my right to state subjective fact, and duly began this account.

SOON, I WILL LEAVE MY room and proceed to the euthanarium. There my short life will be terminated.

I consider the most joyous occasions of my life so far: when Rodriguez 89 passed me the proscribed object, and later, alone in my cell, when I read of that other, wondrous world. The thrill was greater even than that of sex.

Until that time, I had, truly, never known what it was to be alive.

This much I accept: I am guilty. I do not dispute the charge. I do, however, contest the nature of the crime with which I am charged.

And now that I have admitted my crime, I will compound it by stating that which I have never had the courage – or the knowledge, until I read the book – to say before.

I am Daniels 347, and I am a *woman*.

WITH THIS BREAD

TONY BALLANTYNE

DIANA GOT A 60% STAKE in my body the day after my 39th birthday. It turned out that all of those delicious p-burgers I'd been eating had been made up of copyright proteins. All perfectly healthy of course: DIANA's R&D team had simply found a way to insert a custom amino acid every few spaces in the chain and that had been enough to give them rights over the whole molecule. I'd been eating the p-burgers at least once a week for the past five years and my body had been happily using DIANA proteins to replace its own.

All this was explained to me in a polite email sent courtesy of U-be-U, a private health insurance specialist that monitored the bodies of consumers that pass a certain income threshold. I clicked the link in the message and found myself speaking to the severely pretty Dr Deborah Humphries.

She sat in an office made entirely of wood, with a honey varnished maple floor and a rich beech desk and matching chair. Everything about her suggested money, money, money, from her neatly cut dark suit to her time-is-money low maintenance hair style to her money talks Rolex Oyster.

"Ah, Mr Charles Lang." She sounded as if she had been looking forward to speaking to me all morning. "Good to hear from you. You prefer Charlie, right?"

"Er, that's right, Debbie."

"I prefer Doctor Humphries. Now, I see from our files that you have allowed DIANA to gain a 60% stake in your body."

"That's not too bad, is it?" I asked.

She shrugged. "Not as the law currently stands. There is a precedent in Alabama and some of the South American countries for DIANA to have rights over organs built predominantly from copyright protein, but those are unusual cases." She gazed directly at me. "For the moment, at least." She allowed her words to hang in the air.

"But how can that be? They're my organs. They're shaped by my genes."

"Basic law, Charlie. You can't copyright an idea."

"What's that supposed to mean? Since when was my body an idea?"

"As far as insurance law is concerned, it's an act of God."

I stared at her, lost for words.

"...now, let's get down to business. We can offer you a range of health plans that will allow you to regain control of your body at a price that suits your budget."

"Okay?" I said, weakly.

"Our Platinum Service will arrange for clones of your organs to be grown out of material copyright to you and transplanted to your body as soon as possible." She frowned. "Of course, you may find our Silver Service more to your financial situation."

"What does that involve?"

"Consumption of a high protein shake that will rapidly replace the copyright material."

"That sounds like less hassle."

"Ah yes, but you do leave yourself open to possible changes in the law for a longer window of time."

"What changes in the law?"

Dr Humphries looked up at the ceiling and began to recite.

"The EU is maybe eighteen months away from allowing compulsory purchase of organs that can be shown to be medically necessary. The US? Maybe fourteen months."

I realised I had been patting myself as she said all this. Feeling my organs, my own precious organs. Organs that DIANA might just be eighteen months from selling...

"Let me have a look at the Silver price."

"Here we go. There is a finance option available."

I looked at the figures. I could afford it, but only just. It would mean downgrading the car lease, downsizing the property I rented. The trip to Japan would have to be put back another five years, but who had time to take a holiday nowadays?

"I'll think about it," I said.

"Just a warning, Charlie. I can only hold those prices until the weekend."

She broke the connection.

Of course I'd only have until the weekend to decide. There was always a rush, always this pressure to spend spend spend.

That's when the urge rose up inside me, as it always did when I was stressed. The urge to look at the alternative.

I hesitated. What if my boss found out? It was instant dismissal, looking at the outlawed literature…

But at times like this, a person needed to check all the options…

I pulled out the brochure. It was cheaply made, the colours not quite right. The ink had a habit of sticking to your fingers. But the brochure held a picture of another life.

The Northern Enclave. The Outsiders.

The brochure had pictures of people living in the unreconstructed land, north of Manchester. The land that had been razed to the ground by Pina Org in their bold scheme to remake the country. Just before the crash…

Now the Northerners lived a medieval existence beyond the Orgs. They built their own houses, they wove their own clothes. Who would want to go back to living like that? Cold and dirty, and always just short of starving? Growing your own food, burying seeds in the ground and digging up turnips and potatoes and cabbages, boiling them to make potage, just like your ancestors had done.

How long would I have to live on potage before my body was my own?

I gazed at the brochure for another few moments before folding it up and hiding it behind my whiskey collection.

I looked at the bottles, amber liquid glowing in the light. There was another economy. Cut down to one bottle a month from the Vintage society. Regain my body in 12 months.

That was the civilized thing to do.

DIAMOND DOUBLES

ERIC BROWN

THE DISAPPEARANCE OF THE NOTED science fiction editor Dan Woolover around the 10th October 1966 was a cause of great mystery, as were the other disappearances in the area of Tubb Street, Brooklyn, around the same time. However, recent letters discovered at Mr Woolover's office might shed light on the affair.

~

T. Traveler,
22 Tubb Street,
Brooklyn,
New York.
24th May, 1965

To: Dan Woolover,
Diamond Books,
1121 Avenue of the Americas,
New York,
N.Y. 10037.

Dear Editor,

Please find enclosed the ms of my first novel *Life in 3065*, at 45,000 words, for your consideration. I think it would make a very creditable companion to a novel by a 'Bigger Name' in your Doubles line of paperbacks. It's an account of everyday life in the year 3065.

Yours in anticipation, T. Traveler.

~

15 July, 1965

Dear T. Traveler,

Thanks for letting us take a look at your novel *Life in 3065*. After careful consideration, we've decided to pass on this one. While we thought the writing of a high calibre, and the characterisation well done, we considered the novel lacking in plot. Please try us again.

Yours, Dan Woolover

~

25th August, 1965.

Dear Dan,

Many thanks for your encouraging note, a rejection though it was. Please find the ms of my novel *Life in 3075*, at 40,000 words, for your consideration. I've taken note of your critique and made this one a little more plotted, including a sub-plot about a murderer.

Yours in expectation, T. Traveler.

~

11th October, 1965

Dear T. Traveler,

Thanks for letting me see your novel *Life in 3075*. Again, neat characters and the writing is strong... but by plot I mean a progression of events that flow from the consequences of actions taken by the protagonists in the course of the story. What we have here is a mere list of things done by the central character – and what was all that about a strain of altered humanity which feeds off its fellow man? Cannibalism is a big no-no with our readers. To give you some idea of what we're looking for, pick up *Vengeance from Vega* by Philip E. Low, available now from Diamond Doubles.

Yours, D. Woolover.

~

10th December, 1965

Dear Dan,

Many thanks for your letter of the 11th October. I'm sorry you did not care for my realistic depiction of life in the year 3075. I took your suggestion and bought a copy of *Vengeance from Vega* by Philip E. Low, and while I did enjoy the gosh-wow sense-of-wonder plot, I found the novel less than satisfying. For one thing, in the year 2567 Vega will not be colonised, and a race of blue toad-like creatures will certainly not eradicate the colony and then invade Earth. I found this aspect of the story highly unsatisfactory.

Meanwhile, for your edification, please find enclosed the ms of my third novel, *Life in 3085*.

Yours in apprehension, T. Traveler.

~

20th February, 1966

Dear T. Traveler,

I'll give you this, you're prolific, and persistent.

Look, we're a SF imprint publishing action-adventure novels. Your novel, which find enclosed, is frankly more mainstream than SF. Merely writing a travelogue set in the year 3085 and listing a few neat labour-saving gadgets – and the antigrav elevator is a non-starter, by the way: antigrav is impossible – doesn't make the novel science fiction.

In our novels we want space-going heroes who show the aliens what's what, a fast-paced plot, and a happy ending.

Feel free to send us something containing all of the above, and I'll be a happy man.

Yours, D. Woolover.

~

25th March, 1966

Dear Dan,

I'm sorry you didn't care to take my fourth novel, which I thought my very best.

In my fifth novel, *Life in 3095*, which is even better than my last one, I take an in depth look at society and customs in that year. I've taken your suggestion and written a more plotted account of life in the future.

Trusting you will like this one...

Yours in continuing hope, T. Traveler.

~

2nd May, 1966

Dear T. Traveler,

Please find enclosed the ms of your novel *Life in 3095*. For all the reasons stated in previous correspondence, the ms is not what we're looking for. And why this pre-occupation with cannibalism?

I'd be grateful if you desisted from sending us any more of your work.

Yours, D. Woolover.

~

5th June, 1966

Dear Dan,

I am most offended by the tone of your last letter.

I would like to take this opportunity to state that your opinions expressed in your previous letters of rejection betoken not only an inability to appreciate fine literature, but to foresee future trends. Call yourself a SF editor!

For your information (and I have been keeping this fact to myself in previous letters, for fear of earning your ridicule) I have first-hand experience of life in the fourth millennium, as I hail from that era. Hard though it will be for you to credit, I was born on the 1st of May 3055. In the year 3099 I made the unfortunate error of embroiling myself in an escapade that was deemed by the authorities to be less than legal. I was sentenced to mandatory time-transference – to wit, transportation to the Cretaceous Period, there to live out a short life alone while I bewailed my crimes. However, I can only assume that the chrono-sling developed a malfunction, and I found myself stranded – happily – in the year 1965.

Being possessed of a way with words (according to my AI-instructor) and an acute memory, I elected to earn a crust – as I think you say – penning Science Fiction novels.

I very much regret that you do not possess the ability to recognise talent when you see it.

And for your information, antigrav-elevators *are* possible – and will be invented in 2075.

Yours in disappointment, T. Traveler.

~

29th July 1966

Dear T. Traveler,

Now there's a story! It has everything – crime, punishment, devices gone wrong, unintended consequences. Hogwash, of course – but just what I'm looking for! Write it up as fiction in 40,000 words, with added spice – ie, love interest and aliens – and you've got yourself a contract.

And as for you hailing from the fourth millennium… Look, buddy, I get all sorts writing for my outfit: nutty university professors, hacks with delusions of grandeur, and would-be messiahs. I don't know where you fit on that list, but if you say you're a time-traveler from the fourth millennium, that's fine by me. Just so long as you produce the goods.

Yours, D. Woolover.

~

30th August, 1966

Dear Dan,

Please find enclosed the ms of my SF novel Stranded in Time, at 39,000 words, for your consideration. I've 'spiced it up' for the market, and thus consider it far from my best work.

But, as they say, needs must...

And I must register my displeasure at being placed in the same category as nutty professors and hacks with delusions of grandeur. One day, perhaps, I will be able to prove the veracity of my claim that I hail from the fourth millennium.

Yours, T. Traveler.

~

23rd September, 1966

Dear T. Traveler,

Hot-diggety! *Stranded in Time* has everything. I loved the scene where the hero was flung back in time with his broad sobbing buckets and the Tau Cetians in hot pursuit. Great stuff! This is just what we're looking for.

Please find enclosed the contract for $750; sign both copies and return.

Publication is slated for around March next year, and we're putting you back-to-back with *The Two Headed-Thing from Antares* by John Racket. And how about this for a strap-line: *'He paid for his crime by being stranded in time!'*

And if you're ever in the neighbourhood, drop by – I'd love to meet you, Mr Traveler.

PS – One thing… You said you were flung back in time for the error of embroiling yourself in an 'escapade that was deemed by the authorities to be less than legal'. I hope you don't mind me asking just what your crime was?

Yours, D. Woolover.

~

4th October, 1966

Dear Dan,

I'm delighted to have placed a novel with you at last, and I look forward to its publication with anticipation.

You made an assumption in your last letter that I must hasten to correct. You presumed I was 'Mr' Traveler. However, you were wrong. I am not a male of the species… and furthermore – and this might surprise you – nor am I technically speaking a female. We have come a long way, in the fourth millennium, in the science of genetic alteration, and several years ago I elected to undergo genetic-somatic-chromosomal modification. For your information I resemble a human being only from the head up (which makes passing for human in this age not too difficult); however, from the neck down…

Well, perhaps you would care to drop by my apartment one evening, Mr Woolover, and see for yourself.

And my crime? I think that would be better discussed over a few drinks, don't you?

Yours in great anticipation, T. Traveler.

DEAR BURGLAR

TONY BALLANTYNE

Dear Burglar

I thought this note on the mantelpiece might attract your attention. There's a letter for you on the little table by the sofa. It will be in your interest to read it right away!

Yours
Alphonse

~

Dear Nick

Now that wasn't right away, was it? But I suppose I can understand you looking around the room, trying to see if I was watching you.

Well, I expect you want to know what's going on. To find out, head up the stairs and enter the room on the left. There are two envelopes on the desk there. Yours is the pink one, the one on the left. On no account open the yellow envelope!

Best
Alphonse

~

Nick

You had to open this envelope, didn't you? I knew you would. (That should be a clue to what's going on, by the way.) I suppose it was mean of me to hide a razor blade here, but you can't say I didn't warn you. Anyway, before you open the pink envelope, you'll want to attend to that wound. Go to the bathroom (back down the hall on your right). I've left some TCP and a box of plasters on the sink. And next time be careful. I've left more than just razor blades lying around this house...

Yours
Alphonse

~

Hi Nick

Make sure you throw the paper in the bin when you've fixed your hand.

And wipe this message off the bathroom mirror! I expect my house to be tidier than I left it when I return from my holiday!

Alphonse

Nick!

If you'd opened the pink envelope first you wouldn't be standing there with a plaster on your hand. But we both know that was never going to happen, was it? Anyway, by now you should have realised that I know what you're going to do.

So, who am I? Well, perhaps you've heard of me: Alphonse the Mystic. You might have seen my stage show, or you may have seen me on TV, back in my heyday in the '80s. If you have you'll know something about my act. I read people's fortunes. As you may have guessed, my act isn't some sort of trick. I really can see the future. Rather, I can now. Back when I started, it was all just a deception, but you pretend to do something long enough, and suddenly you find you can do it for real. That's what happened to me, anyway.

Now, how clever are you? Clever enough to wonder why I didn't just call the police? After all, if I knew that you were going to break in, why didn't I just have the Old Bill waiting for you?

It's not that difficult to work out. People will accept a stage act, but someone who can really see the future? I don't want to draw attention to myself.

But that's enough from me. It's time for you to leave!

Speak soon.

Alphonse

~

Dear Nick

That's the thing about being clairvoyant. I just know the exact day my mail will be delivered if I put a first class stamp on it. So, you've just arrived back at your flat, you've seen the letter addressed to you and you recognise the handwriting. You've realised that you can't get away from me.

So, what now Nick? Well, let me tell you a little bit more about myself. You'd think it would be pretty neat, being able to see the future, wouldn't you? Not really. Not when you can see the point in the future when your wife was going to cheat on you. And your second wife. And your third one. And your girlfriends. Someone once pointed out that's actually down to my personality and the sort of person I choose as a partner. Maybe they're right. I don't care any more.

You'd think that it would be easy to make money, a few bets on the horses...but the bookies soon get to know you. You're accused of all sorts of things. Yes, I was on TV, but that didn't last.

Apparently I've no charisma. I'm not the sort of person you warm too. As my last wife put it, I've always relied on my good luck, I've never had to bother getting on with people.

She may well be right, but that doesn't alter the fact the last divorce wiped me out.

...and then I see you coming along, Nick. A professional burglar, and a good one at that. So I don't bother changing the lock on the back door, I make it nice and easy for you to get in my house. Call it a test, an interview. Well, you passed. You're going to work for me now. With your skills and my knowledge, we're going to make a great team. Trust me on this. I can see the future.

Okay, you're going to have to remember this, because you'll need to burn this letter when you've read it.

74 Oakland Drive, Mapplethorpe, August 11th to the 25th.

The family will be away in Florida for two weeks. There's a great collection of jewellery in the main bedroom. Lift up the floorboards under the dressing table to get at it.

I'll be in touch later to tell you how we're going to split the loot.

Okay, burn this letter now!

Alphonse

~

Dear Nick

Sorry to hear that you're in prison. I hear that someone alerted the police to your presence in the house you were burgling. Still, I'd never agree with you that burglary is a victimless crime. Even if the items taken have no sentimental value, even if the insurance pays out, there's still that feeling of violation.

And besides, I learned long ago that material goods are not the way to happiness. You shouldn't listen to people who say otherwise, they're rarely telling the truth.

Best wishes
Alphonse

STATE SECRET

ERIC BROWN

ON HIS SECOND DAY IN the White House, the President of the United States of America finished meeting his advisors, discussed policy with a senator from Texas, then braced himself for the encounter with his Chief of Security.

There had been rumours. What he would find out, on ascending to the Oval Office, would make a fricassee of his grey matter. What had the outgoing President said at their last meeting? "Jeez, pal, are you in for an awakening!"

The man to do the awakening was striding through the double doors now, a chunky CIA clone in a black suit. His crew-cut looked as if it had been painted on the dome of his bullet head.

"Mr President, sir."

"Let's get this over with, hey, and then we can all get down to business."

"Fine by me. I'll get straight to the point. There are secrets, sir, and there are secrets. Some secrets are more secret than others."

The President tried not to smile. "Go on."

"Some secrets," said Security, "are for our ears, and eyes, only."

"By 'our', you mean…?"

"I mean, sir, yourself and the usual suspects with security clearance. Plus the physician who made the discovery."

"The physician?" The President echoed. "Discovery…?"

Security said, "We are not alone."

The President made a show of looking around the room. "We aren't?"

Not amused, Security lifted a finger and pointed heavenwards, looking almost angelic. "Extraterrestrials," he said.

The President's first reaction was to laugh. "Little green men?"

"You might say that, sir." Security smiled tightly. "Only they're not green."

We are not alone, the President thought. He'd heard mutterings from a senator out Oklahoma way who'd had it on good authority from high-ups in the Air Force…

His heart was thudding.

"And we have proof?"

"Proof positive," said Security. "We have their ship."

"We have…? Their ship? Roswell, right?"

Security shook his Head. "Their… arrival was more dramatic than any Roswell, sir."

"It was? Then why the hell didn't we know about it?"

Security remained unsmiling. "We did. Every man, woman and child on the planet."

The President said, "Tunguska, right? The Siberian explosion in–"

Security just smiled, shaking his head.

"Their ship wasn't destroyed, sir. Just badly damaged. In fact…" Security turned his finger hellwards. "We have it right here. In a secret vault under the White House."

The President blinked. "Isn't that a crazy place to keep an alien vessel?"

"It makes sense from a security point of view, sir."

The President nodded. "Yeah, I suppose it does."

"If you'd care to take a look?"

"Lead the way."

They left the Oval Office and paced down a red-carpeted corridor, turned right and made for the rear of the building. They came to a steel elevator door. Security jabbed a code, the door sighed open, and they stepped inside.

The doors closed and they plummeted.

The President felt tense. He glanced at Security. "You realise what this means, of course? The advantages we could gain…"

Security faced forward, unsmiling.

Wouldn't life on Earth be irrevocably altered by this…this *proof* that sentient life existed out there? What benefits, scientific, technological, cultural, might accrue from being the first people to contact an alien race?

"We have communication with the extraterrestrials?"

Security cleared his throat, but remained otherwise silent.

Something occurred to the President. "Just when was the ship discovered?"

"Over forty years ago, sir."

Forty years? Then why, thought the President, had the country not benefited?

"And its crew?"

"They died on impact – all but one being. It managed to communicate before it too expired."

A minute later – longer than the President expected – the elevator bobbed to a halt. The doors eased open.

They were in another white-painted, red-carpeted corridor. They paced along the corridor and came to a door like that of a bank vault.

Security turned the swivel wheel and hauled open the door. It came slowly, revealing an aseptic chamber. Side by side they stepped through the door. Security ushered the President across the ringing tiles to another vault-like door and swung it open.

The President entered, looking around for the alien ship. He saw nothing. The chamber was empty.

"This way, sir." Security led the President over to what looked like a viewscreen set into the wall.

The President stared through it, and saw, seemingly floating in the air, a torpedo-shaped vessel in three crumpled sections. It was hard to discern the craft's true size.

The President shook his head. "I take it we're in contact with the aliens' homeworld?"

He saw that Security was shaking his head, almost sadly. "That isn't possible, sir."

"It isn't? But–"

"The physician who discovered the ship, sir, spoke with the surviving alien. It apologised for what it had done, once the physician had explained the situation."

"*Apologised?*"

"The being then contacted the orbiting mothership and suggested that no further contact between our species be attempted, for fear of human reprisal."

The President opened his mouth to speak, but Security went on, "The alien died soon after, before the physician could assure the alien there would be no reprisal, and that contact between the races would be welcomed." He shrugged. "We haven't heard from them since."

"But…" the President said. "What did the aliens do to fear our reprisal?"

Security held a hand up before the screen. "Take a closer look, sir."

The President peered, and it was as if an optical illusion had suddenly resolved itself. The screen was not a window into another room, but a container like an aquarium set into the wall.

And, within the container, the extraterrestrial ship was revealed to be the size of a cigar butt, perhaps an inch long.

"Apparently it went out of control when entering Earth orbit and broke up on impact. There was no way the crew could have avoided what happened. It was just… bad luck."

The President said, "Just where did it come down?"

Fearing the answer, he leaned against the wall to steady himself and stared at the alien vessel.

It looked for all the world, he realised now, like a bullet.

"Dallas," Security said, "on the 22nd November, 1963."

His head reeling, the President pushed himself from the wall and hurried from the chamber.

THE STARS ARE FALLING

TONY BALLANTYNE

THERE ARE STILL PLACES IN Atlantis that feel like they were made only yesterday, but there are fewer and fewer of them all the time. In a few months there will be none, and the whole island will assume a mask of antiquity.

But that could be said of the whole world, of course: the artificial stars are falling one by one from the skies, and the eyes of the people are falling with them as they turn their gaze downwards and inwards.

I ARRIVED AT THE LITTLE port feeling not only tired and dizzy, but also with a growing conviction that we'd made the wrong decision in coming here in the first place. The feeling had first arisen when I heard that the airport had been disassembled three months ago; the runway gone the way of Cape Canaveral and Star City, the ground ploughed up and seeded with pottery fragments.

Sally met me as I climbed from the boat.

"Good to see you back," she said. "I've a little welcome present for you."

She pushed something like an egg into my hand. Strong yet fragile, cool but strangely warm. "It's an Atlantean pot."

"Oh yes?" I turned the pot back and forth in my hands, noting the way the patterns seemed to move beneath the fresh shine of the glaze.

"Do you like it? They researched the clay that would make up our island and then ran thousands of hours of simulations to come up with that colour."

"It's wonderful."

"There's very few of them left now," she said, thoughtfully. "We smashed most of them up and buried them."

I cupped the pot in my hands, thinking about the magnitude of what we were trying to achieve.

"I know," she said, seeing the expression on my face. "It gets to me like that sometimes, too."

She turned and began to walk away.

"Come on," she called over her shoulder, "you're in luck. We've still got the use of a couple of cars. They're not being removed until the end of the month. I've requisitioned one to take you to the camp."

We climbed into the car, and she drove us across the artificial island that was being restored to a past of the imagination, a past that had been constructed in the last three years.

SALLY DROVE THE CAR ALONG a bumpy road. The grass had been allowed to grow through the widening cracks in the surface.

"You'll want to see the library, now that it's finished," she said.

"Oh yes!" I said. "I always regard the library as being the heart of what we're doing here."

"You won't hear any disagreement from me," smiled Sally. "I'm a linguist, and this island is built on language."

It was my turn to smile. "I think the construction team might have something to say about that."

I remember when the island was nothing more than a cooling mass of magma ejected from an induced fault, the yellow constructor ships had hovered overhead with a hungry air as if they couldn't wait to get started.

"Well. I suppose the weavers and the potters were working before us, but the language underpins everything that's been done. Here we are…"

She brought the car to a halt. Seen from outside, the library was an elegant domed and white marble faced building. Inside it seemed larger than expected, the interior was formed from a series of concentric stone circles stepping down to a central ring. If you didn't know better you'd have sworn the stone had been cut thousands of years ago, that it had spent millennia beneath the waters. I'd been wondering about the books. How were they going to explain the fact the paper had lasted so long?

I beamed as I saw the answer.

"You made the books from ceramic sheets? That's brilliant!"

It certainly was. What better way to explain the preservation of knowledge when Atlantis was "rediscovered"?

She opened a book, turned it proudly so I could see the pages.

"They chose logograms, as you can see. I'm told there are over ten thousand of them, though they've only used about three thousand of them in the finished artefacts."

The logograms were beautiful: balanced and spare, graceful swoops and trails…

"They're drawn with a blade. You take a piece of wood and carve the end into the shape of something a bit like a chisel. You dip that into the paint and then as you turn it on the surface you can create all sorts of shapes. That one there means harmony…"

I placed a finger on a shape made of three balanced curves. It made me feel at peace just to look at it.

"You've done a fantastic job," I said.

Stood there, in the middle of the library, the sun peering through a series of lemon marble arches as it set, the sea air blowing in my face… Just for a moment, I believed. I believed that this place had once existed, that people had built it and lived here long, long ago. Sally saw it in my face.

"I know," she said. "We've done a good job, haven't we?"

"Magnificent."

She swallowed. There was just the tiniest hint of pleading in her voice. So small you barely heard it…

"A better way of spending money than rockets and satellites, isn't it?"

She would say that, of course. This was her field. But maybe she had a point. There had been the accidents in space, of course, lives had been lost, but that wasn't the reason for Atlantis. That wasn't the reason we'd built the island. After all, people had stopped seeing the benefits of space travel before they'd stopped believing in the future.

"Maybe it is," I said. "There's always been a balance between those searching for a mythical past, and those looking to a possible future."

And maybe when we'd poured our resources into looking outwards we'd failed to communicate what we were doing to those still here on Earth. And now the power cuts were blanking out the city lights and the night sky was clear and filled with more stars than I could imagine. All of Earth's gifts were being returned to Earth as humankind brought its works back home. The deserts of Australia and Africa were full of ships and satellites, all being disassembled. Earth was retreating in on itself…

But we still needed to hope. People still needed a glimpse of a better world…

I'd agreed to it. But just then, the sight of the heavens rising up and up was enough to make me falter. Just what were we giving up?

"Do…do you think we've made the right choice?" I asked.

"It's the right choice," said Sally. "The time for looking outward has passed. It's time for us to look inward. We've made our own culture to study. Humanity can strive for eternity by looking to itself."

And now we'd shut the door on space. It would be hard to open it again.

"We can look to ourselves, can't we?" she pleaded.

"We'll have to," I replied.

GUNS-U-LIKE

ERIC BROWN

IT'S THE DAY AFTER USA went to the polls and the NLP has won the people's vote. Bands play in the street and crowds cheer. The Democrats have been soundly beaten and a new dawn is under way.

Chuck Goodfellow lies on the shrink's couch. His face is bruised, with a nasty cut just above his right eye.

"And how are you feeling today, Chuck?"

"Not too good, Doc, to be honest."

"I'm sorry to hear that. Now, the last time you saw me…"

"I don't want to talk about my childhood!"

"I understand. I understand completely. Now, why is that?"

"I don't like thinking back, you see. I get uptight."

"I understand. But… you've never to me about your parents, Chuck."

"My parents?"

"Your father. Would you like to talk to me about your father?"

"Not really."

"Why is that, Chuck?"

"He was a perfectionist."

"In what way?"

"Whatever I did, it wasn't good enough."

"In what way, Chuck?"

"Well, y'see... he set me chores, and I goddamned did every last one of them, and then he'd inspect what I'd done... and jeez, but I was shit-scared. 'Cos every time he'd find something wrong."

Chuck falls silent, his eyes glazed.

"And what then, Chuck? What would your father do?"

Chuck shifts uncomfortably. "I don't want to talk about that, Doc."

"Why not, Chuck?"

"Because... I just don't."

"What kind of relationship did you have with your father?"

"Relationship?"

"How did you get on?"

Chuck shrugs. "Not too good."

"Did he beat you?"

After a long silence, Chuck says, softly, "He'd unbuckle his belt and pull it from his waist-band real slow, smiling all the while."

"And then?"

Almost inaudibly, Chuck murmurs, "And then he'd lay me over a chair and whip me. Six times. Twelve if he was feeling real mean."

"And what do you think about that now?"

"It makes me feel angry with my pa, Doc. Real angry. I mean, I never got a chance to show what I was really made of. He never give me a chance."

"Do you see your father these days?"

"Pa's dead. Took his Smith & Wesson and..." Chuck shakes his head. "He killed himself, Doc."

"And how did that make you feel?"

"I felt real swell at the time. Went along to the cemetery and damn near danced on the old bastard's grave. These days... these days I wish..."

"Yes?"

Chuck shrugs. "I dunno."

"Do you wish you could confront your father, Chuck?"

"Confront him?"

"Talk to him?"

"Yeah. Yeah, that'd be good, real good."

"And what would you say?"

"What would I say? I'd say..." Chuck falls silent, frowning. "I dunno."

"Think about it, Chuck. Imagine your father, standing in front of you, saying nothing, just listening to what you had to tell him. What would you say?"

"I'd say... I'd just say, 'You never listened to me, pa.'" Chuck shakes his head, staring into space. "He never let me have my say."

"Your say?"

"About my anger. I still have that anger, Doc. I feel... I feel as if there's a monster inside of me. A monster just waiting to get out. Sometimes the anger just swells up inside and it's all I can do to stop myself from… from…"

"Yes?"

"I have these fantasies, Doc. It's me against the world. I mean, I didn't ask to be born, did I? I don't want to be here, most of the time. I mean, nobody gives a damn about me. Women just look right through me, and men are no better. I get beat up a lot, Doc. I don't know what it is, but I seem to invite these big fuckers to come along and…"

"Ah, I see… the bruises. Who did that?"

Chuck shrugs. "I dunno. Some bastard I bumped into in a bar."

"What happened? Did you start it?"

"Me? God, no. This bastard… he just started mouthing off, calling me… calling me names. Then he hit me. I tried to fight back. I tried real hard, but I'm no fighter…"

"You mentioned having fantasies."

"I'm not proud of them."

"Tell me about your fantasies."

"They're real mean fantasies."

"Tell me about them."

"Okay, so there I am, walking down the street. I'm in a crowd of folk. There's lots of couples, men and women, holding hands and making out… and I'm alone. Like, you never feel more alone than when you're in a crowd, do you, Doc?"

"That's very true, Chuck. And what do you do?"

"In my fantasy I'm armed, see? I'm packing this Beretta semi-automatic and I'm itching to use it. I'm real itching to use the piece. And then I see my mom in the crowd."

"Your mother?"

"I know, I know… It's screwy 'cos mom's been dead these past twenty years. She took an overdose after Pa walked out. But anyways I see my mom, and she's telling me what she always told me, back when I was a kid. That I'm a no-good little shit and I'll never amount to anything."

"And what do you do, Chuck?"

"What do I do? I pull out my Beretta and aim at her head and I pull the trigger and I watch my mom's brains hit the wall behind her, and I watch her fall to the ground and I wish…"

"Yes?"

"I wish it was my father I'd just killed. But there's this fat old dude standing over mom's twitching corpse and he's staring at me, hatred in his eyes – just like my pa stared at me. So I raise the pistol and shoot him dead. And… and you know what, Doc? It feels good, real good. It's like I imagine sex to be. I feel powerful, and respected, and I keep on firing into the crowd, wiping the hatred off all the faces, and I'm feeling better all the time, the more people I stiff, and I'm thinking, if only my pa could see me now."

"It's okay, Chuck; it's okay. It's only a fantasy. You're fine now. Deep breaths…"

"Sure… thanks, Doc. You know, talking helps. Helps a lot."

"That's good. That's why you're here, Chuck. Letting it all come out makes you feel better. That's good."

"Thanks, Doc. I mean… I don't know what I'd do without you, you know?"

"That's okay. That's what I'm here for, after all."

Chuck watches his shrink as he makes a few notes on his pad.

"So… what do you say, Doc?"

"Are you sure, Chuck, that you're taking your medication?"

"I'm sure, Doc. I'm taking the pills. All of them."

"Good, Chuck. That's good. Now listen to me… I want you to go to the clinic directly and ask to see Dr Robinson. She'll talk to you, assess your medication and maybe make some adjustments. I'll ring through and arrange an appointment for you straightaway, okay?"

"Sure, Doc. Whatever you say. And thanks. Thanks, Doc. I appreciate everything you're doing for me."

"That's what I'm here for, Chuck. Take care."

"I will, Doc."

"Goodbye, and remember. You go straightaway and see Dr Robinson."

"I'll do that. So long, Doc."

CHUCK GOODFELLOW LEAVES THE CONSULTING room, takes the elevator to the street and steps into the crowd celebrating the election win. He walks along the street, buffeted by folk whooping and hollering. A marching band passes beneath a red, white and blue NLP banner, and Chuck stands and watches all the happy faces. He remembers what he told his shrink about crowds, and he sees men and women embracing, perfect strangers meeting and hugging and celebrating their party's victory.

He thinks about going to see Dr Robinson and thinks, *what the hell…*

A blonde kid beams at him, a NLP worker. She thrusts something at him and yells, "Your lucky day, sir! We're giving away a hundred free vouchers…" She goes on, her words lost in the scrimmage of folk fighting for the remaining vouchers.

Chuck reads the leaflet, then reads it again, and he smiles as if all his Christmases have come at once.

"Well, what do you know?" he says to himself.

He's got himself a seventy per cent reduction on small arms at the downtown Guns-U-Like store.

He pushes through the crowd, turns down a side street and approaches a taxi rank.

"Guns-U-Like," he says to the driver, "and step on it!"

It's the day after USA went to the polls and the National Libertarian Party has won the people's vote.

THE CLEVEREST MAN IN THE WORLD

TONY BALLANTYNE

"Hi, this is Clark Maxwell, the cleverest man in the world. Ten seconds, ten thousand euros. Off you go!"

"Clark! My name's Bob. My parachute's broken! What should I do?"

"Hi Bob. Let me see. GPS has you twenty thousand feet over Arizona. That's pretty high up! Given a terminal velocity of a hundred and eighty feet per second, you've just under two minutes before you hit the ground."

"I know! What do I do?"

"That's a tough one! Give me a minute to think…"

"What? No! Don't hang…"

Too late. Clark checked the volume of space around Bob on his computer and switched to the next call in the queue.

"Hi, this is Clark Maxwell, the cleverest man in the world. Ten seconds, ten thousand euros. Hit me!"

"This is James Sunderland, CEO of eToys. Clark, we've got a spy in the company. Every new product we develop, our competitors get to market weeks before we do."

"Spies aren't your only problem then, you must be very inefficient in terms of product manufacture."

"Oh. What should we do?"

"That's two questions, James. Just give me a second…"

Clark called up eToys on a second monitor. Keeping one eye on Bob's rapid descent, he ran a couple of searches in quick succession.

"James! You'd have had the answer yourself if you'd taken the trouble to check your network audit trails. The plans are being deliberately downloaded onto games cartridges as part of the background scenery. Your competitors are buying your secrets wholesale. Now for your second question, may I suggest that you make an appointment with my PA to discuss looking at your company from top to bottom."

"Uh, sure. Thanks, Clark."

"Don't mention it. Bob! How's it going?"

"Still falling, Clark."

"I see that. Bob, I want you to look down. Do you see the big lake?"

"Yes. Should I aim for it?"

"No! But don't you find it beautiful? Calming even?"

"No. Should I?"

"Back soon, Bob… Hi, this is Clark Maxwell, the cleverest man in the world. Ten seconds, ten thousand euros. What's the problem?"

"This is Lewis. Can't seem to get a girlfriend, Clark."

"Hmm. That's because you're so self obsessed. Get a hair cut and start paying attention to someone beside yourself."

"Hey, can you see me?"

"No. Never seen you in my life, Lewis."

"Then how do you know that's true? About the haircut and everything?"

"You've got ten thousand euros to spare and you're using it to ask a stranger how to get a girl. Anyone who thinks that money solves all their problems is probably pretty self obsessed. Time's up!"

"But…"

Clark tapped at his keyboard.

"Hi Bob! I can see you now."

"How?"

"I've taken control of the plane you jumped from."

"Can you do that?"

"Did I mention I was the cleverest man in the world? Hold it Bob, I'll be back in a minute!"

"I don't have a minute!"

"Hi, this is Clark Maxwell, the cleverest man in the world. Ten seconds, ten thousand euros. How can I be of service?"

"Clark, this is your wife, the smartest woman in the world. Have you walked off with my car keys again?"

"Sorry, Lois. Will you be home tonight?"

"Assuming I get the super collider fixed. I think I know what's causing the problem. It's not its future self it's interfering with, it's its past self."

"Sounds cool, dear. Got to go! Hi, this is Clark Maxwell, the cleverest man in the world. Ten seconds, ten thousand euros. Hit it!"

"Clark, this Tessa Walkiewicz, Acronym news. We're doing a report on the acceleration of change and we'd like a few words…"

"Certainly, Tessa. Just a moment… Bob, you're falling too fast. Hold your arms and legs wide. I'm sure you've seen people do it in films!"

"It looks easier in films, Clark."

"I know! Just do your best! Marianne is jumping out of the 'plane, right now. She's got a spare chute for you."

"What 'plane?"

"Your 'plane, Bob. The one you jumped out of. It's right behind you!"

"Oh! That's clever!"

"That's my job…back in a moment, Bob. Tessa! What's the question?"

"Well, Clark. Given the growth of the internet and the new paradigms of interconnectivity, people such as yourself are emerging as a powerful force for social change. Plugged into the world's data streams, you have a view of everything changing from minute to minute."

"That's not a question, Tessa."

"No that's an intro, Clark. The question is this: given that people are using services such as yours more and more, does that mean they are getting less intelligent?"

"I hardly think that many people are using my service, Tessa. Not at the prices I charge!"

"Maybe not yours, Clark, but given that the answer to any problem you have is only a phone call away, why should people think for themselves any more?"

"Let me turn that around, Tessa. When they stop thinking, they stop being people. Got to go!"

"But…"

"Hi, this is Clark Maxwell, the cleverest man in the world. Ten seconds, ten thousand euros. I'm listening!"

"Uh, Clark, this is Marianne. I jumped out of the plane, I've attached myself to Bob."

"Well done Marianne! What's the problem?"

"It's my chute. It's failed to open, too. The ground's looking awfully close."

"Marianne, thank you! I do like a challenge! Now, listen to me carefully…"

TERRORTORY

ERIC BROWN

HE WAS IN THE FIELDS when the terror descended.

He heard a roar and turned to see a cloud of dust rising in the distance. He set off at a run towards the village, his stomach frozen with fear.

On the way he met the first of the refugees, dazed and bloodied and crying in despair.

Where his village had stood, a sheer black wall now rose, seamless and seemingly infinitely high.

He walked again, this time into the mountains. Along with other refugees, he climbed.

He looked back, and saw that the wall was a monolith, one of many such dominating the landscape.

Hours later he turned again. This time he made out more gigantic blocks, striding across the desert towards the distant capital city.

They created arcane shapes which vanished into the mist, spelling out the name of a country in a language he did not understand.

Together with his people, powerless to resist, unable to understand, he climbed.

AN (ALMOST) TRUE STORY

TONY BALLANTYNE

"WHERE ARE WE GOING?"

"It's a surprise."

I was driving my two friends, Steve and Chris into Manchester. They were wearing leather jackets and jeans, I was in my fleece and chinos. Gig gear.

"Who are we going to see?"

"You'll find out when we get there. This is my treat."

I pulled off the road onto the parking strip outside the row of shops at the bottom of the Oldham Road, just down from the Chinese Hypermarket. The edge of the city is lit up in orange streetlights at that time of night. It's a no-man's land, washed in headlights, alternatively filled with sound of traffic accelerating as the lights change, and then near silence as the traffic recedes into the night.

"Hah! We're going to the Band on the Wall," said Chris.

"Genius," said Steve. "Where else would we be going, parked here?"

We entered the club via the new entrance, a glass atrium on the side of the old hall. There's a bar at the back selling the sort of drinks you never used to see at this sort of club.

"So, who are we seeing?"

"Possibly my favourite singer-songwriter ever…" I said. He's up there with Joni Mitchell, Paul Simon, Hoagy Carmichael and all the others I can't think of as I write this.

"Lost your tickets?" laughed the man on the door as I patted my jacket.

"Found them!" I said, pulling them out. "What time's he on?"

"Eight."

We went straight in and sat down, second row back from the stage. A piano stool, a mic, and a collection of effects pedals took centre stage.

"We're here to see Chris Smither." I looked around the room. Fifty years in the business, and judging by the number of seats set out, he would be playing to a crowd of around eighty. There's a pleasure in being in the know, but it didn't seem right that there were so few people present.

We didn't have to wait long before the man himself walked onto the stage. No MC, no introduction, he carried his own guitar onto the stage, said hello, sat down and began to perform. I should say now, by the way, that if you want to know what Chris Smither sounds like, well, he's on YouTube. This isn't a review, nor is it that literary device that I particularly detest: a description of the music. You want to know what music sounds like, listen to it.

No, this story is about my feelings on attending the concert. Because a story is all about communicating emotion, and to me, this was like meeting an old friend. I've watched Chris Smither perform all over the country for the past twenty five years or so. Odd to call him a friend, because I doubt he knows who I am: we've spoken briefly about half a dozen times and that's it. But, just jumping ahead, when I spoke to him at the end, we both remembered the gigs he used to do at the Half Moon in Putney. I think there's something storylike in the way we both live completely different lives and yet we connect infrequently in different venues, far from both our homes.

But back to the concert. Steve, Chris and I listened to the first half.

"What do you think?" I asked as the artist took a break and went to sell some CDs next door.

"Wow!" said Steve

"He's very good," said Chris.

"He's seen life. There's a wisdom to his songs…"

"Just imagine," I said, "just imagine that he was a modern day messiah, going from town to town, preaching the truth."

"He's not that," said Steve.

"I know. But just imagine that he was. If I'd heard what he sings when I was seventeen…"

"If you heard him when you were seventeen you wouldn't have listened," said Chris. "You've got to have lived your life to understand what he's singing about. You've got to have already made those mistakes to understand his advice."

He had a point. I only ever listen to advice after the event.

ONE LAST THING.

Someone requested that he play a song called Hold On. He began the song, but had to stop half way. It was his own song, his own arrangement, and it wasn't working. As he explained, it had been a while since he'd performed it, and if you don't practise them every day, you quickly forget them. This from an expert musician who performs live to an audience many nights of the year.

There's a lesson there somewhere.

AESTHETIC APPRECIATION ON ASPEREX

ERIC BROWN

I WAS FOUR WHEN THE aliens came.

They arrived in a silver ship. We watched it land in the desert and squat there, silent and menacing. As the hours elapsed and nothing happened, we gained confidence and moved ever closer, until there were thousands of us surrounding the otherworldly vessel.

I WOULD HAVE BEEN FIVE that day, but for an unfortunate accident. I was exploring a sinkhole in the desert, a deep well that had never before been plumbed, when my organ of Aesthetic Appreciation slipped and fell to its death while admiring a particularly striking rock formation.

My Tactile and Locomotive organ dutifully made its way down the sinkhole and retrieved the corpse. I trudged homeward, bearing my dead organ, and on the way encountered a citizen who challenged me. I would have fought, but, incomplete, was compelled sadly to stand down.

Once home I broke the news to my mate, who offered the temporary services of its Aesthetic Appreciation organ. Though flattered, I could not accede to what I considered (somewhat prudishly, perhaps) a perversion.

I contacted the Completion Bureau and made a formal request for the introduction of a new organ of Aesthetic Appreciation. The citizen in charge informed me that I might have to wait a month for my request to be processed, and then another month until the appropriate organ was located.

I tried to watch holo-vis, but even my favourite show, *Soaring with Suss in the Stratosphere*, failed to evoke any sense of wonder. My mate and I left the burrow and strolled through the desert, all nine of us (how sad that sounds!), and watched rock-hoppers mating in the twilight. The activity would have normally left me replete with wonder at the beauty of our homeworld, but that night it moved me not at all.

"Perhaps two months without Az…" (Az was the pet name for my late organ of Aesthetic Appreciation) said my Cognitive and Computative organ. "How will we manage?"

"Life will be reduced for the period," said my Gustative and Digestive organ, and suggested a consoling feast of sand-snakes when we returned to our burrow.

Duly I watched my Gustative and Digestive organ consume fifteen live and writhing sand-snakes, then we linked and Gus (as it was known affectionately) digested the snakes and passed on the nutrients. The death of Az made even the appreciation of the meal somewhat jejune.

"I know!" declared my Sexual and Reproductive organ. "We should initiate congress with mate. That might assuage our loss."

So I called my mate and suggested congress, and we linked, the nine of us, and our Sexual and Reproductive organs slobbered and sucked and wrestled each other. But though my mate could not withhold its obvious delirium, I was unmoved. I feigned elation, but feared my mate had seen through my duplicity.

In a bid to distract me, my mate suggested a hunt. I assented, and we left the burrow and watched, with some mild amusement, as our Tactile and Locomotive organs ran down and ripped apart several sand-burrowers.

The following day, the aliens arrived.

THE DAY PASSED WITH NOT the slightest movement from the silver vessel.

"To think," said my mate as we stood before the ship, "that there are others in the universe like us, intelligent beings come to test us!"

But while I could appreciate on an intellectual level the import of the aliens' arrival, any visceral appreciation was sadly absent.

Towards sunset a hatch opened in the side of the ship and a being emerged, but even then I felt only a stirring of mild curiosity. The creature was bizarre, to say the least: it was merely tripartite, with each organ oddly resembling the other.

The being spoke, though only later, our scientists having studied computers within the ship, were the words made public. "We come," said one of the being's as yet unidentified organs, "from planet Earth…"

The organ fell silent as our clan leader approached. I must admit that I felt, then, a surge of passion as I watched our representative – five proud, strong, linked organs – take a stance of confrontation. Its organs addressed the alien in concert, "We welcome you to Asperex," and it made the appropriate invitatory gestures.

The alien must have had extraordinary translation equipment, for duly one of its organs moved away from the ship and approached our leader in the established mode of conflictory acceptance. (I assumed they had been studying our cultural mores for some time).

On the ship's ramp, the two remaining organs were communicating with each other (though the content of their speech has become evident only recently). "They look like lobsters, but the ugliest lobsters I've ever seen. And… what's it doing? My God! It looks like it's pulling itself apart. Each section has eyes and… Oh, Jesus! Martin – run!"

But the organ that had accepted our leader's invitation to fight merely stood there, as if frozen, and collapsed upon the onslaught of our leader's Tactile and Locomotive organ.

The remaining organs turned and retreated within their ship – and duly we took the invitation to follow up our victory. Verily these creatures were ill-equipped in the field of inter-species conflict! We swarmed *en masse* aboard the vessel, located the remaining aliens and rendered them limb from limb, in the accepted fashion.

Tales are still told, all these years later, of the time we had aboard the alien ship.

The vessel stands, somewhat weathered and rusted these days, out there in the desert – a monument to our glorious first meeting with beings from another world.

And my tale has an even happier ending. Some three months after the events I have described, the Completion Bureau contacted me with the happy news that a prospective Aesthetic Appreciation organ had been found.

We were united at an official ceremony three days later – and oh! the world then seemed a wonderful place!

We made a pilgrimage across the desert to the alien ship. We completed the customary circuit, while my Cognitive and Computative organ narrated the events of that wondrous day – and the latest addition to my self, my adopted organ of Aesthetic Appreciation, allowed me to take in the true sublimity of first contact.

And I wept.

PLENTY MORE FISH IN THE SEA

TONY BALLANTYNE

"OH, SHE'S GORGEOUS!" BREATHED KARPAX. "Just look at that carapace."

She looked just like Karpax to me, a two metre tall insect covered in horribly prickly hairs. Her main arms were long, ending in human-like hands, the second pair were smaller and sported a pair of pincers.

"She's coming over," I said, watching her push her way between the tables in the crowded bar. It was full of spacers from all over the galaxy who had met to drink or inhale or imbibe or engulf or whatever else it was they did to relax and let off steam. Humans like myself were definitely in the minority.

Karpax was running his hands through the bristly hairs on his abdomen, releasing a faint but extremely unpleasant aroma to mingle with the pungent air of Midway Station. So many alien races meeting in one place leads to an exotic atmosphere.

"What should I say?" he asked.

"Nothing," I advised.

"Hi," said the female insectoid. "My name is Xaralee. And you are?"

"Karpax."

"I'm Steve," I said, in businesslike tones. It made no difference, she only had eyes for Karpax.

"Tell me, what's such a handsome Insectoid doing here on Midway?"

"Just taking a rest before taking our cargo on to Gernsback."

I kicked him under the table.

"Hauling a cargo?" she said. "What do you carry?"

Karpax was falling under her spell by now, but he still retained some vestige of cunning.

"Nothing special," he said. "You know. Stuff."

"Stuff?" she said. Her translator did a superb context mapping of a playful giggle. "Oh, that sounds so interesting. I just love stuff."

I drained my beer and slammed the glass down.

"Come on, Karpax. We have to get back to the ship. We need to look after the stuff."

"I know," he said, getting up to follow me.

"Will I see you again?" asked Xaralee.

"I hope so," said Karpax.

I DIDN'T SAY A WORD until we were back on the ship. We stood in the hold, looking at the cargo. Bottles and bottles of yellow royal jelly, all bound for Gernsback.

"What was the matter with you?" I asked. "Couldn't you tell she was a spy?"

"I guessed," said Karpax, sorrowfully. "But she was so pretty."

"So what? I don't understand how you can let her play you like that. You know that it's not you she's after."

"No, you don't understand," snapped Karpax. "Insectoid females can alter their body chemistry. They tailor their pheromones to the mate they're trying to attract."

Actually, I knew that already, but I was still irritated. I got the feeling he just wasn't trying hard enough to resist her.

The computer spoke up and broke the awkward silence.

"There is a guest outside. Would you like to invite her onboard?"

A viewing field opened up in the middle of the hold.

"Xaralee!" cried Karpax, excitedly.

"Get a hold of yourself," I said, and immediately wished I hadn't.

"We should let her in," said Karpax.

He would say that, of course. But an idea occurred to me…

"Why not?" I replied. "Computer! Open the airlock!"

I met Xaralee in one of the rooms we inflate outside the ship's hull when we need to receive visitors.

"Hello," she said, looking around the room. "Where's your friend?"

Wordlessly, I looked to where Karpax had just entered the room.

Xaralee turned to face him, her hairs bristling as she pumped pheromones into the air. All of a sudden, the hairs relaxed.

"Karpax," she said. "Why are you wearing a spacesuit?"

"I've just been outside."

She flashed me a look that I didn't need a translator to interpret. When she spoke again, it was in a wheedling tone.

"Oh, Karpax. I can't see your lovely face in that suit. Or the way your body gleams in the light. Take it off for me!"

"You're just saying that so you can get at the cargo!" Karpax sounded hurt, now that he could see he was being used. "You've just been stringing me along so that you can get the royal jelly and turn yourself into a queen. Well, forget it, sister. We've got our reputation to think of. People trust us to keep their cargo secure."

Xaralee span to face me.

"This was your doing, wasn't it?" she said. "You've done everything you can to break us apart!"

"Let's have a little perspective here," I said. "You only just met him an hour ago."

I had to hand it to her, she kept her dignity.

"Be like that," she said. She turned her back on us, ready to flounce out. "Your loss, Karpax. Don't bother to call me. There's plenty more xargs in the methane pool."

And at that she left the ship, her hairs bristling again. I hadn't noticed until then, just how pretty those hairs were.

PLENTY MORE XARGS IN THE methane pool? We would say plenty more fish in the sea. How true that is.

Karpax found me a few weeks later. Tracked me down to a small bar on Aspen's World.

"I knew I'd find you here," he said. "What happened to the ship?"

"Xaralee sold it," I replied. "She needed the money to build a hive now that she's a queen."

Karpax sighed. "I should have guessed. Look, I'm sorry it took me so long to get here. It took forever for me to hitch a ride, once you took off without me. But never mind that. Come on, we're leaving."

"Leaving? Why should I leave? This is my home now, here with my Xaralee, my love."

Karpax sighed and held something out to me.

"What's that?" I asked.

"A spacesuit. Put it on, Steve. We need to talk…"

CHILDREN OF EARTH

ERIC BROWN

I WAS IN THE BATHROOM, helping my daughter clean her teeth, when the aliens arrived on Earth.

Ella insisted on grabbing the toothpaste. "I don't need your help, Daddy. I'm four now. I'm a big girl!"

"But don't get too much—"

Too late: a great slug of stripy paste slopped across the bristles of her toothbrush and onto the floor. "Oops…"

"You see. Now let me help."

"No!" She pulled away, glaring at me. "Mummy says I'm a big girl now. I can do it!"

I smiled and watched her try again. A medium-sized blob of toothpaste emerged and by some miracle landed on the brush.

"See!" she beamed, delighted.

I'd left the TV on in the lounge. "We interrupt this programme to bring you breaking news…"

"Daddy," Ella said through a mouthful of toothpaste.

"Mmm…?" I was straining to hear the news report.

"Why do you think you can do *everything* for me?"

"Because I'm much older than you, darling, and more experienced."

From the lounge I heard, "… just one hour ago a vast floating ship appeared over Hyde Park…"

I moved from the bathroom and stared at the screen. An opalescent oval vessel, so vast it blotted out half the sky, hovered over the park and slowly descended. My legs suddenly weak, I slumped on to the sofa.

Ella bounded into the room, a book tucked under one arm, and plonked herself on my lap.

She stared at the TV and sighed. "Mummy says you watch too much sci-fi, Daddy."

"Mmm," I said. Fiona, my wife, was working a late shift at the hospital and I wondered if she was near a TV. What would she make of this? She'd always derided my hope that, one day, we'd be visited by extraterrestrials.

"Daddy?"

"Hm?"

"I'm hungry. I want supper."

"But you've just cleaned your teeth!"

"I know. But I'm hungry."

"Okay," I said. "I'll fix you a sandwich and some warm milk."

"I can do it!"

I imagined the resulting chaos if I let her. "No, I'll do it." I could see the TV from the kitchen.

A reporter was babbling, "The ship has landed! A vast crowd is converging on the vessel. Police are powerless to stops citizens getting close…"

I poured a glass of milk and put it in the microwave.

Ella was on the sofa, leafing through her book. The TV showed the milling crowds around the alien vessel in Hyde Park. The microwave beeped and I took the warm milk out and finished making a marmalade sandwich. I carried everything through to the lounge and sat beside Ella.

"Now," she said, "tonight, Daddy, I will read to you."

I nodded. "Good."

She began reading about a little girl left home alone for the day and all her messy adventures.

"A portal is opening in the flank of the vessel," the reporter cried. "A ramp is descending and… and, yes, I can see movement within the craft!"

I stared at the triangular hatch in the silver flank of the starship, my heart pounding. A shadowy figure appeared.

"Ella," I whispered. "Look at that… An alien. Aliens have come to Earth, and you were here to see it happen."

I looked down at her, but she was too absorbed in her book. She was reading to herself, her lips moving silently.

The alien emerged from the vessel and paused at the top of the ramp. It was small, childlike, and garbed in a one-piece overall that reminded me of a romper suit.

A small silver sphere floated above the being's left shoulder.

The extraterrestrial raised its right hand in greeting. It spoke, and a second later the silver device translated its words.

"Greetings, children of Earth," it said. "We come to your world in hope that we can assist you with the benefit of our experience."

Ella giggled at something in her book and I pulled her close to me.

BALANCE SHEET

TONY BALLANTYNE

I NEED TO DRINK A bottle of whiskey a week to help me cope with the stress of my job. I like the good stuff, so that means I spend sixty pounds times fifty-two, what's that, £3,120 per year on whiskey. Count that as a necessary expense of the job, and I do, and it means that you can subtract £3,120 from my yearly income. So I don't make quite as much money as first appears, but I still earn more than you do, and I get to drink good whiskey every day.

I SUPPOSE I HAVE TO mention the real minus. Write this in the ledger in big red letters. My soul is held as collateral by something nameless. Security against a loan of money that I used to set myself up in the business.

Some people would swap their soul for the certainty of a good life. Forty years of port and cigars, fine leather coats and the gentle purr of an expensive car. Women in New York and Paris. Women in Tokyo for that exotic touch.

Not me. Oh, I wanted all that, don't get me wrong; it's just that I was willing to work for it.

I took the modern approach. A little pain, a little gain. Call it a timeshare. A little time spent elsewhere once a month, either for the next forty years or to the end of my natural life. Whichever comes first. And that's it. After that period my soul is my own, and I keep what I've made for myself with the money.

So there you are. I get all this. The house, the car, the women, the respect, all for a little trip elsewhere once a month.

I DON'T EVEN GET NERVOUS in the time leading up to the trip. I thought ahead and ensured that was part of the deal. Everything is a little hazy. After all, a life lived in fear is a life half lived, eh?

IS THIS SIN? A BLASPHEMY? I don't know. Don't talk to me about blasphemy. My first wife and son were killed by some drunk in a car crash two years before I signed that deal. If we can sin, then what does that say about the power that let that arsehole jump the light and smash into the side of my car? And then in court she dresses up in a smart grey suit and talks some crap about depression and gets off with a fine and a two-year ban. Where's the justice in that? How can He justify that?

Don't talk to me about blasphemy.

IT'S THERE IN MY DESK diary now. Thursday 14th March. 11: 50pm. A little red rectangle on the page. Seven days' time.

You've got to take risks, but you've got to be sensible too. Always read the small print. Better than that, learn to listen to what's not being said. If someone comes up and offers you what appears to be a solid business opportunity, just think to yourself, what's in it for them? If it seems too good to be true, it probably is. Sit back and examine the deal from all sides. Don't be blinded by the positives, look for the negatives. I learned that long ago. Suckers want to be conned. They want to believe they're getting a good deal.

So when I got offered this little deal I was man enough to look at the plus side and the negative, and I saw the catch. And I swung the deal to my favour.

I don't remember anything about it once I'm out of there, right?

Right.

I MAKE VOICE NOTES ON my phone, you never know where you're going to get an idea. Tracy writes them out for me each night.

Here's a funny thing. The ones relating to you know what don't get transcribed. It's like Trace doesn't hear them, but if I rewind, there they are. Makes sense I suppose. They don't want other people knowing about them.

THREE DAYS TO GO. I do wonder what it's going to be like for that brief hour when they own me. I do think about it in the last few days leading up to it. I admit it. The worst pain I was ever in was after the car crash. Not so much the dull ache of my bruised arm, or the knifing agony from the whiplash when I moved my head, no. It sounds stupid, but it was the injections they used to give me. I'm frightened of needles. The sight of that gleaming steel tip, a little clear fluid oozing from the end. The smell that you get from the alcohol they soak the swab with, that squeaky feel of the cotton wool on your skin just before they push the needle in.

I'm shaking here just describing it.

I guess they use needles on me. Strap me in a machine, needles in my arms, needles in my legs, needles in my eyes. I read somewhere there's this thing they do to check for some sorts of cancer, stick the needle right into the bone. They can't anaesthetise bone, apparently. You lie there and feel the pain, you listen to the crack as they force the needle in.

I think that's what they do to me.

IT'S ONLY FOR AN HOUR, and I don't remember it afterwards.

IT'LL BE HAPPENING IN EIGHT hours' time. I got a call on my mobile ten minutes ago.

"Mr Johannsen? Just a reminder about your 11:50 appointment this evening. I trust everything will be in order?"

"No problem," I said. "I will see you then. Usual place?"

"Usual place."

It's like making an appointment for the dentists'. An unpleasant little necessity.

YOU'RE LOOKING FOR SOMETHING BAD in my life, aren't you? Something else on the balance sheet that would help you equate your life to mine. Something that would help you to feel that bit better about yourself. Okay. I'll tell you.

I miss my wife and boy. We always thought that we'd stay together.

But these things happen. You can't change the past.

11:49 AND I'M WAITING IN my lounge. Got the TV on, 60 inch widescreen, sound coming out of the Bang and Olufson. Glass of whiskey in my hand.

I've got that feeling of anticipation like you get at the dentists'. I feel like the time I went to have my tonsils out; that wait in the hospital bed before they come around with the premed. I'm drunk on whiskey. I can see the images on the TV moving back and forth. Some late night crap. Men with guns and women half out of their clothes. That sort of low-grade pornography they play for people too embarrassed to admit that's what they want to watch.

A man appears from the corner of my living room. Stepped out of somewhere else, just standing there next to the blonde bookcase. He's dressed like a salesman. Cheap suit and sad moustache. Bad haircut and dandruff on his shoulders.

"Mr Johannsen?" he says.

THE WALL BEHIND THE MAN has vanished. One of my lounge walls is missing. There is the wooden floor, the white walls and then nothing. Just this brown orange mist like street lights on fog. A high-pitched whining begins, the sound of a dentist's drill.

I feel like I'm going to shit rusty water, but I force myself to speak.

"I'm coming," I say, struggling to get out of my chair. I reach for the whiskey.

"That's okay," says the man. "You just stay there. You never come in, you just watch."

"Oh, Okay." I say, relieved. I slump back into the chair and drink the whiskey, and peer into the fog, intrigued. What's going to happen? Something is moving forward. A small shape.

It's Geoff. It's my boy. His eyes are wide and his mouth is twisted and there are tears everywhere and he is crying and crying in a shrill voice that is filled with pain and desolation and he's looking at me with an expression of utter betrayal, shrieking and shrieking, "Daddy, Daddy. You promised, you promised, Daddy…"

And in the background I can hear someone else screaming and sobbing it's my wife

"Oh no please, please not again, no…"

…and Geoff looks into the mist and then back at me and his face is twisted in horror and misery.

"…Daddy please, you promised you'd make them stop…"

1:15AM AND THE ROOM RETURNS to normal. The man dressed as a salesman hands me a glass of whiskey. Memory's a bit of a blur. I'm having trouble thinking straight.

"Same time next month, Mr Johannsen? Or would you prefer to cancel the arrangement now?"

"What? Arrangement. Yes. Something about the arrangement…"

"I'll just take the phone, Mr Johannsen. Got to erase the naughty bits…"

FIXATION MORBIDITY

ERIC BROWN

SO... TODAY IS WHEN I edit myself.

I should be through in an hour, maybe two. I have a lot to get rid of.

It's a process I go through every fifty years. The medics at the Institute warned me of the consequences should I miss a wipe.

I'm doing it for my mental health.

I glance into the kitchen. Mr and Mrs DuBois, from the agency, are sitting at the table, drinking coffee and waiting patiently.

So here goes.

THE DEVICE LOOKS LIKE A silver skullcap, with a chinstrap to keep it in place once it's activated.

I place it on my head, fasten the strap, and activate the control in my right hand. I'm aware of a faint buzzing at first, and then a pleasurable warmth passes through my head.

Dr Evans appears before me, seated in the recliner. He's smiling. "Good to see you again, Ed. Are you ready to go?"

The image of Dr Evans always makes me sad. He's a hundred and fifty years dead, now. Ironic, isn't it, that one of the medics to work on the project at the Institute, in the early days back in 2150, was unable to undergo the treatment and in consequence died when he reached his allotted five score.

"I'm ready to go," I say.

"Very well." He looks down at the screen in his right hand, then smiles up at me. "I'm getting high scores – way up in the nineties – for some emotional trauma dating from 2284 and emanating from someone called Ola. Shall we take a look?"

"Let's do that," I say.

THE SIMULATION IS MORE VIVID than my memory.

I'm at the party where I met Ola, forty years ago. We hit it off immediately. She's tall, blonde, Scandinavian, a violinist with the Swedish National Orchestra. We have a love of classical music in common. We meet again a week later, and after that are inseparable for two years.

We marry in 2282, and it's downhill from there.

Dr Evans appears, overlaid on a stilled image of Ola arguing with me at breakfast.

"Okay…" he says. "She was a bad choice, Ed. You should never have gone there. I've warned you off the domineering, alpha-female types before, and taught you how to spot them. But you keep on ignoring me, even though you know I'm right, and even though you know how dangerous it is for you. It's that oedipal thing again, Ed."

Despite myself, I groan.

"So," Dr Evans says, "I suggest we Wipe, agreed?"

"Agreed."

"Let me see…" He refers to his screen and nods. "That's the two years you were together, and thirty-eight years of consequent memories." He taps the screen a few times, murmuring to himself. "Laying down the tracers, implanting the erase command. Commencing the Wipe in five, four, three, two, one… Now."

I wince in anticipation. A fierce heat blasts through my head, a synaptic firestorm. I rock in my chair, cry out loud – and then it's over.

And I feel great.

Whatever emotional trauma was lingering in there from the memories of whoever or whatever were wiped from my consciousness has now cleared, and I feel clean, refreshed… *renewed*.

"Are you ready to go on?" Dr Evans asks.

"Let's do it!"

"THE NOVEL YOU WROTE IN 2265."

"That failure!"

The simulation shows me the office of my publishers, and the grim face of my editor.

Dr Evans says, "It's laying down a whole seam of trauma and negative associational emotions. Wipe?"

"Wipe!" I agree.

The simulation vanishes.

I brace myself. The firestorm, and then release...

"Your unfinished twenty-third symphony...?"

"I don't know... Dah-di-di dah-di-dah! It means something to me, on a level I can't access. Maybe one day I'd like to finish it."

"I wouldn't advise that, Ed. According to the data-stream..." He consults his screen again. "The symphony is responsible for a certain fixation morbidity. I'd advise we Wipe it."

He continues with the psycho-babble, and convinces me.

"So Wipe it!"

He Wipes, and after the firestorm I feel much better – though, of course, I have no idea why.

"2275. The death of your youngest daughter..."

I weep. He doesn't need to lay down a simulation. My memory provides everything. Lizzie had just celebrated her 102nd birthday and was driving home with Vince, her eleventh husband. The auto-drive malfunctioned and the safety baffle failed at the same time, and the car ploughed into an oncoming fifty-tonne juggernaut. Lizzie and Vince were killed instantly.

Killed dead.

Dead *forever*.

"Wipe!" I yell.

Firestorm, then relief.

"2278. YOUR NEXT WIFE, JAN—"

"Wipe!"

"2285. CLIVE, YOUR THIRD HUSBAND."

"That bastard? Wipe!"

"2286. THE BUSINESS DEAL WITH Amalgamated Assets?"

"Wipe."

"2287. ELSA SIMM—"

"Wipe!"

"2288. CLIMBING MOUNT—"

"Wipe!"

"2289. YOUR MARRIAGE TO BOB and Maria—"

"Wipe!"

"2291. THE TRIP TO MARS—"

"Wipe!"

"2292. YOUR TENTH NOVEL—"

"Wipe!"

"2293. THE CANBERRA OPENING—"

"Wi…"

"2298. THE HOLIDAY IN PARIS–"

"Wah…"

"2299. CHRISTMAS EVE–"

"…"

NICE MAN SMILES AT ME.

"That brings this session to a close, Ed. Mr and Mrs DuBois will be on hand for the next few months to take care of your every need. Don't worry about a thing. You'll be back to normal very soon. Don't cry, please don't cry… I'll see you again in fifty years."

Smiling nice man and woman take off my hat.

"There, there, Eddie. Let's go to the bathroom, hm? You've been a naughty little boy and we need to clean you up."

Giggles. "Wipe!"

RONDO CODE

TONY BALLANTYNE

"I REMEMBER, I WAS TEACHING kids how to program computers. I was trying to think of ways to make it easier for them. The thing is, they have no trouble writing lists of instructions; what they find difficult to understand is the looping and the branching…"

Ada broke off as the sound of an orchestra sprang up and the whole world paused. The traffic in the road by the little pavement café, the pedestrians, even the birds in the lime trees. Somewhere up in the sky, aeroplanes hung motionless for a moment. And then their courses adjusted slightly, the music came to an end and the world resumed. Everyone relaxed. Four days since the big glitch, and everything seemed back to normal.

"You understand what I mean?" she said. The journalist opened his mouth to answer and she interrupted him. "Of course you do now, but before all the changes, this is what kids used to struggle with."

Ada had taken a dislike to the journalist. He had arrived at the interview with his mind already made up. She was amusing herself by not giving him a chance to speak.

"Like you can draw a square by repeating four times the routine go forward ten steps and turn right ninety degrees. That's an example of a loop. Kids used to struggle with that. Adults used to struggle with that.

"So I was trying to think of a way to help people understand. I was listening to kids singing The Twelve Days of Christmas, and I thought that's really quite complex: in the old jargon, the song is an example of nested loops. You count from one to twelve, first day of Christmas, second day, yes? And then for each day you have to count backwards to one: Seven swans a swimming, six geese a laying, five gold rings. I thought, that's not a song, that's a code structure.

"I thought, they understand songs, maybe I could teach them to code that way. That's when I came up with the idea of Rondo Code."

She sipped at her drink.

"Why's it called that?" asked the journalist, free to speak at last.

"Rondo Code? I thought everyone knew that by now, Mr Leibniz. A rondo is a musical form. You play tune A, then tune B, then tune A, then tune C, then tune A and so on. It was a catchy name that sort of described what I was attempting."

Mr Leibniz smiled and Ada knew that piece of information was of no interest. He wanted to assign blame. People had nearly died in the big glitch.

"Well, it worked, he said. "Anyone who can sing a tune can now understand how to program a computer."

"It's not just that. Think of all the testing we used to do, all of that debugging. Now you can tell if a program is well written just by listening to it. Does it have musicality?"

"That's an interesting philosophical point," said the journalist. "Are humans programmed to program?"

"It's a silly point," said Ada. "Anthropomorphic thinking. We do what we do."

"Hmm," said the journalist. "But of course, all that was a prelude. Your stroke of genius was still to come."

"Nonsense. Nothing I have done could be described as genius. Rondo Code was a good idea, that is all. There was a lot of hard work went into the syntax and structure. I have shown dedication, nothing more."

"Others might disagree, Ms Byron. Cottrel says your idea to put existing music through Rondo Code was genius."

"Cottrel is a second rate composer, not a programmer."

"Where did you get the inspiration from, Ms Byron?"

"I hate that word, inspiration. If I hadn't thought of the idea, someone else would have."

"But they didn't, Ms Byron." He shook his head in wonder. "Who would have thought it? That Beethoven's Sixth Symphony could predict the weather? Or that Wagner's

Tristan und Isolde could control negotiations between warring states?"

"That program has yet to bring of a satisfactory resolution to a conflict," said Ada, tersely.

"But it keeps both parties in dialogue rather than fighting. You've got Duke Ellington running primary education and Melissa Hui controlling the traffic…"

"I think you're simplifying things for your readers, Mr Leibniz. The music needed some adaptation…"

Leibniz waved a hand, and it was obvious to Ada that those words would never see print either.

"Was it your idea to use Mozart to control well-being?"

Ada was silent for a moment. Here was the blame.

"No. Nor was I the hero who managed to correct the code and allow us all to sleep again."

Leibniz stared at her. He wasn't quite ready to give up.

"Why did you agree to this interview, Ms Byron? You're famous for being something of a recluse."

"I just don't like talking to the press. It may surprise you to learn that's not the same thing."

The journalist laughed.

"So why speak now?"

"I just wanted people to understand. The big glitch is over"

"Hmm." He tapped his pencil on his teeth. "So, my final question. You're not universally popular, are you? It has been said that once a piece of music is put to work as Rondo Code, all the pleasure is taken from it."

"I've heard that said," said Ada. "There are fools in every age."

"But surely, once a piece of music has been reduced to a mechanical series of notes, once it has been fully understood by a machine, surely the pleasure has all evaporated."

"Since when did understanding spoil pleasure?" asked Ada, standing up. "In my experience, it tends to enhance it."

SOME NOTES ON OWNING A HUMAN: TEN BRIEF OBSERVATIONS

ERIC BROWN

1) HUMANS MAKE IDEAL PETS, but to get the most out of your Human you must be prepared to put in a little hard work. Remember, dedicated effort in the early stages of a relationship with your pet will result in a Human that is obedient, affectionate, loyal – and ultimately productive.

2) HUMANS WERE NOT ALWAYS so amenable. In the early stage of contact between our species, Humans proved to be aggressive, mendacious and untrustworthy. They displayed the contradictory characteristics of individualism bordering on arrogance and an almost obsessive clan loyalty. We found that they were not to be trusted either as individuals or when collected under the banner of states or nations. However, measures laid down five millennia ago to neutralise their natural aggression, combined with sustained corrective discipline, has resulted in a race which is docile, biddable and –

despite being of limited intelligence – able to learn within certain parameters.

3) THE BEST RESULTS ARE achieved if you obtain your human when it is young. Teenage humans can make good pets, but the amount of training required – to correct errant ways learned in the wild – is not conducive to a modern busy lifestyle. Obtain your pet from a certified hunter or breeder when the Human is between the ages of three and five. Be warned that Humans do not thrive in isolation. If you have time, ensure that your pet shares a living space with you or your hive-mates. If the latter proves problematic, it is *not* advised to obtain two Humans; instead, show your Human more affection. (See point 5, below.)

4) IT IS ADVISED THAT one hour a day should be allotted to training. Humans can learn basic verbal commands, and have the ability to understand simple concepts and retain upward of two thousand words. Rewards for comprehension should take the form of small edible treats. Fruit is ideal. A simple command followed by physical instruction, repeated a dozen times, will have the desired effect. Within one month you will have a Human who will understand a wide range of instructions and be able to converse with you on a simple level. (It must be remembered that a Human's capacity for abstract thought is limited: they are not a philosophical race, and for instance do not comprehend the Seven Higher Laws or even the Three Fundamental Concepts. In the early decades of

contact, Humans displayed an aberrant desire to profess belief in an Almighty Deity, though this absurdity has been bred out of them.)

5) HUMANS THRIVE ON AFFECTION. It is advised to maintain physical contact with your pet whenever possible; caressing with pseudopods, grooming with ancillary tongues, and enfolding in lower limbs has been shown to produce excellent results in terms of engendering loyalty. Some owners maintain that sexual congress with one's pet is another way to sustain an individual's obedience; personally I do not find myself attracted in this way to my Human (whose name is Campbell) though several of my hive-clan are predisposed to such liaisons with it.

6) BE ADVISED THAT AT the age of approximately fourteen Terran years, your Human will undergo sexual awakening (though if you have practised sexual congress with your pet before this age, then its awakening might be consequently accelerated). It is advised that you allow your Human to mate with another Human at regular intervals throughout their adulthood – though cohabitation with another Human is not recommended as this might lead to issues such as disobedience and diminution of loyalty. To prevent unwanted births, it is strongly advised that your pet should be rendered infertile at the time of purchase.

7) YOU MUST BEAR IN mind at all times that your Human pet does not think as we do. It is a mistake to ascribe to your pet the characteristics and attributes of our own race. For instance, behaviour that indicates intense pleasure in you or I – such as Prolonged Intensive Screaming – does not denote the desire to communicate joy, as with ourselves; in humans this behaviour is indicative of distress, anger, or pain. Likewise, behaviour like prolonged physical activity (such as running) does not mean that your pet is predisposed to mental breakdown. In humans, such seemingly pointless athleticism is required for mental and physical well being. (For other examples you are advised to consult my treatise *Understanding Human Psychology*.)

8) IT IS INCUMBENT UPON an owner not only to train one's pet but to teach it. Before contact with our race, Humans had achieved a limited sentience and a rudimentary form of civilisation – 1.5 on the Galactic Scale. (They had accomplished limited space-flight, fission technology, and a basic understanding of Quantum Theory. However, this was achieved at the cost of Global Disharmony. When we intervened in the affairs of Humanity, their race was on the brink of extinction. World Conflict raged, and weapons of Ultimate Destruction were within months of utilisation. Only our arrival upon their world prevented Humanity from annihilating itself.) It is advised that at least one hour a day is given over to a simple discussion of Terran history with your pet. This not only encourages basic one-to-one compassion in

your Human, but loyalty. We are, after all, the saviours of their race.

9) AFTER BETWEEN TWO AND three years of Diligent Husbandry, it is predicted that your relationship with your Human will have attained reciprocal affection and respect. Your pet will appreciate all that you have done for it, and you will have gained from your Human the altruistic satisfaction of having aided your pet towards Greater Understanding.

10) WHEN YOUR HUMAN REACHES the age of twenty Terran years, the time of Ingestion and Ultimate Union is nigh. A well-educated Human will give itself willingly to the ritual – more, it will feel privileged to do so. After all, what greater goal could any Human desire but the Ultimate Sacrifice to its master? However, ill-educated or sub-normal Human subjects might bridle at the idea of Sacrifice, and attempt to escape. Such aberrant behaviour cannot be countenanced, and the Human miscreant must face execution and thus forego the joy of Ultimate Union.

In three days I will Ingest Campbell, and my pseudopods shringle at the thought; Campbell, too, is excited at the prospect of its sacrifice. It has been well-educated. Daily it begs me to, "Ingest me now so that I might cast off this terrible illusion."

In closing, I wish you well as you look forward to the time of Ingestion and Ultimate Union with your member of the Human race!

Raha'mahtu-5, Divisional Superintendent of Planet Earth.

COMPATIBILITY

TONY BALLANTYNE

TOMORROW:

"Give me your phone," said Claire, holding out her hand. She was pretty: green eyes and dark hair and a knowing smile. Ewan handed his phone across without any reluctance, but then…

"Hey, what are you doing?" he squawked as she plugged a cable into the base. "Don't flash it! It's still under warranty!"

"I won't harm it. Anyway, if I'm right this will be so worth both our whiles…"

"Why?"

Ewan watched the screen of the phone flicker as the software loaded from Claire's laptop.

"This is called Compatibility," said Clare. "It looks at the music on your phone and compares it to mine, sees how much of a match we are."

"Okay…"

"It's clever, too. You can't just load your phone full of jazz, say, to try and be pretentious or to get on someone's good side. It checks to see how long the tracks have been played. Compares them with the websites you've looked at, all sorts of things."

She tapped at her own phone screen.

"Here it comes," she said.

The sound of the wedding march sounded from her phone and Ewan's at the same time.

"Ahah! See, just as I thought. We should get married right away."

Ewan looked at Clare, just long enough to reassure himself she was teasing.

"I thought maybe a drink first," he replied, struggling to regain his cool.

FIVE YEARS FROM NOW:

They occasionally talked about getting married, but there was never time, and besides, things were so good between them they didn't see the need to get a piece of paper to affirm it.

Clare had just returned from Arkhangelsk when the messages came, two of them arriving simultaneously on both their phones. Ewan was lost playing Hero's Quest, he only looked up when he heard Claire's gasp.

"What is it?" he asked.

"Something called Compatibility 2.0," she said. "It says it's found better partners for both of us."

Ewan pulled out his phone and looked at the profile of the woman suggested. She was called Anka: blonde, Polish. He looked down the metrics.

"I've got someone called Dean," said Claire.

"What's he like?"

She didn't answer. He knew why. Anka's photo was, well, stunning. But it wasn't just that, it was the story written in the data that accompanied it. Everything about her, her work, opinions, hobbies, everything about her fascinated him. And maybe he had been getting bored, and maybe it was time for a change…

"Who do you have?" asked Claire, an edge to her voice.

"She's called Anka."

They looked at each other. Ewan spoke first.

"I'm happy with you, Clare."

"Oh! Good!" She hugged him.

"Are you crying?" he asked.

"…no…"

TEN YEARS FROM NOW:

Ben should be home from school now. Clare would be feeding little Jamie. Ewan knew he should be there to help, to give her a break. But even so, he'd stayed on at work, pushing files from one directory to another. Anything to have a little time to himself.

The message came through around half seven.

Compatibility 3.0.

This woman was called Dinah. He'd never met a Dinah before. She was a buxom red head, she worked a few hours a week in little boutique jewellery shop. The rest of the time was spent in the gym or lunching with friends. They had nothing in common, looking at the metrics. Nothing except for one thing.

She was the horniest looking woman Ewan had ever seen. At that moment there was nothing he wanted more than to plunge himself inside her, to lose himself between those breasts.

And she was nearby, right now. Drinking in the bar of a little hotel, just around the corner.

He looked at the screen of his phone, wondering…

THIRTY YEARS FROM NOW:

It seemed that since the kids had left home they never spoke with each other except to argue. Everything she did was irritating. Everything. The way she never put anything away, the way she left her shoes in the middle of the floor, the fact she wouldn't eat broccoli, or the way she always waited until he was playing a game before asking him a question…

This time he didn't wait for the message to come. He looked up the software on the web: Compatibility Ultra.

"What's that?"

He hadn't heard Clare enter the room. He looked up, guiltily. Guilt, he thought. Why should I feel guilty?

"Thirty years," said Clare. "Two people live together for thirty years. And yes, the grass looks greener. But we've shaped each other, you know."

"Shaped each other?" he said.

"And maybe you pass a point where there isn't anything better, but that's because everything else is so much worse…"

She held up her phone. Ewan saw the Compatibility logo first. And then he registered the picture. Grey, with watery blue eyes. He never thought of himself as looking like that…

He looked down at his own phone, looked at the picture there. It was Claire. She still looked beautiful.

"Bloody software," he said.

"Are you crying?" asked Claire.

"…Got it right first time… Stupid, pointless upgrades…"

REDUCTIO AD ABSURDUM

ERIC BROWN

THE PRESIDENT WAS ENJOYING A leisurely stroll along the beach when he saw a glint of gold in the sand.

"Whoa!" his security guard exclaimed. "Bomb threat."

Security eased the object from the sand and, after a thorough inspection, passed the lamp to the President.

"Looks just like Aladdin's Lamp," he said to himself, and slipped it into his pocket.

That evening, alone in the bedroom of his summer retreat, the President examined the lamp.

Standard issue fairy-tale magic lamp, as far as he could see. Smiling to himself, he gave it a rub.

He jumped back in alarm and dropped the lamp as smoke funnelled from the spout and coalesced into the form of a rather overweight genie.

"Oh, Master," said the genie – *so far so clichéd*, thought the President – "thou has saved me from purgatory. How might I be of service?"

"Hm, it's usually three wishes, isn't it?"

"Three? You have been misinformed. The wishes I will grant you are limitless."

Limitless, thought the President. *This should be interesting.*

The genie said, "What is most important to you?"

The President considered the question. "The security of my beloved country, of course."

"Then I advise that your first wish should be how I might assist you in securing your beloved country."

The President paced back and forth for over an hour. At last he came to a decision. "I wish that my great country existed in a world without al-Qaeda and Daesh and other such terrorists."

"Your wish is my command," said the genie.

THE FOLLOWING EVENING, AFTER A security meeting with his advisers, the President summoned the genie.

"Tell me something," said the President. "The al-Qaeda problem is no more. They've simply vanished – as if they've never been. But not a soul in the world but me is aware of the fact."

The genie smiled. "That is because I excised the memory of al-Qaeda and other terrorists from every mind but your own."

"Very clever," said the President. "But what did you do with...?"

"I gave them an Earth of their own."

Ingenious, thought the President, and got on with running the country.

MONTHS PASSED AND THE RUSSKIES began getting uppity again. The President had forgone the option of using the genie in order to line his own pocket, but once again national security was at stake.

He summoned the genie and said, "Genie, those goddamned bolshie Russians are playing up. I think they should be removed."

"I will attend to the matter at once, oh master!"

And lo! When the President woke up in the morning, the Russian problem was no more.

A YEAR PASSED. THE PRESIDENT had never been so popular, the country never so safe or prosperous.

Came the day when another bunch of no-good sabre-rattlers – this time the Chinese – began to rattle more than just their sabres.

But the President was equal to this threat.

He summoned the genie and announced, "Genie, those darned Chinks need to be taught a lesson once and for all."

And it was done.

THE PRESIDENT SECURED A SECOND-term in office with a landslide majority.

America, policeman of the world, policed a world of relative peace and harmony – notwithstanding the occasional rumpus that was put down with a firm hand.

A year passed and a trade agreement with the Europeans – always a gaggle of cent-pinching bastards – turned nasty. A US battleship was attacked in the Mediterranean; for a whole tense week, the country was in a state of nuclear alert.

To avert disaster, the President rubbed the trusty lamp.

"Oh, master, your wish is my command!"

"I've had a bellyful of those garlic-eating Euros, genie! Away with them!"

"It shall be done."

EIGHT YEARS AFTER COMING TO office for the first time, the President ruled over a vastly depopulated world. In fact, only one country existed on the face of the planet...

There was a problem, though.

Internal division.

Texas wanted independence, and so did Alaska.

They wanted independence so much that they were willing to fight for the privilege.

Not that the President would let matters reach such a sorry state.

Once again he summoned his trusty genie, and once again the genie did his job.

TWELVE YEARS AFTER FIRST COMING to office (the President had changed the constitution to allow himself to run for a third term), the President sat alone in the Oval office.

The past few months had seen a lot of rubbing of that old magic lamp, resulting in the banishment of all those ingrates who had opposed his rule.

The President now governed a few thousand cheerful souls in a post-technological, hunter-gatherer civilisation.

But not everything was rosy in the garden.

There was division amongst the populace.

The Woodland tribe was sore about the Coasters hunting on their sylvan territory.

Something had to be done about that.

THE PRESIDENT OF WHAT HAD once been the United States of America sat on the beach – not a stone's throw from where he had discovered the magic lamp, twenty years ago – and stared out to sea.

He had done a lot of thinking of late. There was little else to do, with no-one to rule over.

Sometimes he got a little lonesome, and on these occasions he would summon the genie and shoot the breeze.

He was becoming dissatisfied, though. A voice in his head was beginning to anger him.

He came to a realisation that he was his own worst enemy, and summoned the genie.

"Genie," he said, "how do I get rid of the voice in my head?"

"Allow me," said the genie.

A second later, the President vanished.

And for the first time in a long, long time, peace reigned on Earth.

FUTURE TENSE

TONY BALLANTYNE

JEAN GLANCED NERVOUSLY AT THE fortune teller. She counted the money in her purse for the twentieth time and told herself she could afford it, just. If she didn't buy herself a drink tonight, if she skipped lunch tomorrow... She wondered again if she was wasting her money. She knew it was just a bit of fun, just some old woman dressed as a gypsy. But Mary had sworn blind that this old woman had the gift. She had told Mary that her son was going to leave home. How could she have known?

The old woman must be genuine. But didn't that make things worse? She should ask about Neil, but could she bear to hear the answer? What if he didn't like her?

She looked back at the fortune teller and then counted her money for the twenty-first time.

"Excuse me? Do you mind if I have a word?"

The words brought her back to Earth with a bump. A grey haired man stood before her table, smartly dressed in a suit and tie. He looked quite out of place in the ballroom of the hotel, stuffed as it was with holiday makers. There was the shriek of children mixed with the gentle chatter of their parents. It was the lazy, slack time of the day when people read magazines and drank aperitifs and waited for dinner. Jean's mother was upstairs having an afternoon nap.

The smart stranger sat down in the seat opposite. Jean put her purse away, grateful for the distraction from her dilemma.

"Can I help you?" asked Jean uncertainly. The man looked important. She felt as if she had done something wrong. The man saw her uncertainty and smiled, a pleasant, friendly smile.

"Don't worry." he said in a rich, fruity voice. "My name is Mr Williams. I'm here to help you."

"Yes?" said Jean. She felt herself become calmer, bathing in the easy warmth of his personality.

"Yes. You see, I tell fortunes. Genuinely."

Jean glanced towards the old woman in the corner. She held a young girl's palm in her hand, her eyes closed.

"Not a charlatan." said Mr Williams. "Not like our good friend over there, dispensing easy platitudes to credulous fools. Not that I condemn her for that, I hasten to add! She brings comfort to those in need. She is a good woman. A good woman, but a fake nonetheless."

"Oh." said Jean. She held her handbag tightly. She had almost been taken in. She felt foolish.

"Don't feel foolish." said Mr Williams. "I'm used to this sort of reaction."

"You don't look like a fortune teller," said Jean, suspiciously.

"So how should I look?"

"Like her," she said, pointing to the woman in the corner.

"That's just a costume. I don't need to look the part, I'm the real thing."

There was something very sincere about Mr Williams. Jean picked up her purse again.

"I'm sorry, I can't afford much."

"I ask for no payment."

Mr Williams took a white handkerchief from his pocket and laid it out on the table.

"Place your hands there, please. Thank you. You must realise, Jean, a true teller comes to those in need. We see the future, we see who needs us. We go to them. What sort of seer waits for clients to arrive at his door? Perhaps the clients don't know they need help!"

Jean was astonished. How had he known her name?

"You think I need help?" she asked, eyes wide.

Mr Williams made no reply. He stared intently at her hands.

"Shouldn't you be looking at my palm?" whispered Jean.

"Shhh. The palm tells only part of the story. I'm concentrating on the whole picture."

The chatter of the holiday makers filled the room. There was the scrape of chairs, the sound of a young child crying. Mr Williams was a dark pool of silence in the middle of the confusion.

"You're here with a relative," he said suddenly.

"Yes…" said Jean. "My mother."

"You have to look after her. She's ill."

"It's her chest…"

"There's nobody else to look after her, you feel it's your duty. And yet… You feel as if you're throwing your life away. You feel like you deserve something more… And yet, you feel guilty about these thoughts."

Jean's eyes widened in astonishment. How could Mr Williams know all this? It was as if he had reached deep down inside of her and stirred her mind. Secrets long hidden were bubbling to the surface.

"I don't mind looking after her," she said, defensively. "What else am I to do?"

"Ah, What indeed? But don't they say, a problem shared…?"

Jean blushed. Had he seen Neil there in her thoughts?

"I wouldn't dare… No. Anyway, who would look after Mother? Not that he would even look at me. We're not teenagers, are we? We're too old for that kind of thing."

She realised she was babbling.

"You're never too old for that kind of thing," said Mr Williams. "Why hasn't he asked you yet?"

"He doesn't even know I exist."

"He does."

"How do you know about him?"

"I can't help knowing these things." Mr Williams smiled, as if enjoying a private joke. "You could say it was my job. Now, the question is, what are you going to do about it?"

"What am *I* going to…" The thought seemed to spin Jean around inside. It had never occurred to *her* to do anything. She had been leaving that up to Neil.

"Come on, Jean. How old are you? You can't be so old fashioned you think that women have to let the man to do all the running?"

"Mother said…"

"Your mother is wrong. We both know that."

They held each other's gaze. Something broke free inside Jean.

"You're right, Mr Williams," she said "I'll do it now. While I've still got the courage." She rose from her chair and left the crowded ball room. She was going to dress for dinner in her nice red skirt and blouse. Tonight, Neil would ask her for a drink after dinner. She'd make sure of it. Neil, who came and sat at the table next to theirs each night, who watched her so shyly and intently and had never quite plucked up the courage to ask her out… Jean felt her confidence rising by the minute.

MR WILLIAMS WATCHED HER GO with a smile on his face. Claire, the waitress appeared at his side.

"You've done it again, haven't you?" she said.

"Yes."

Claire began clearing the glasses from the table.

"You know so much about them, I sometimes think you really are psychic."

"Nonsense. There's no such thing. I just keep my eyes open and tell them the truth. If you want something, you've got to go for it. You can't just sit and wait for it to come to you. I've watched her every day mooning at him in the dining room, and him doing the same back. I saw her sitting by the fortune teller and I knew what to do."

"You'll get into trouble someday."

"Nonsense. This is my hotel. It's the manager's job to keep the customer satisfied."

THE OTH

ERIC BROWN

ROBERTS FIRST HEARD OF THE Karran people in the late 1960s. A geologist at the University of Brazzaville told him about a remote tribe living along a tributary of the river Congo. He claimed that they had only ever seen one white man – the geologist himself. Roberts was intrigued. He made arrangements to travel up country and contact the Karran people.

A year later he did just that.

IT TOOK HIM A COUPLE of weeks to win the trust of these shy, gentle people. He spoke a version of their language, and soon learned the variations of their tongue. They were hunter-gatherers, nomadic, and animist. They believed in a host of nature gods. There was no crime amongst their tribe, and they did not commit violence upon their fellow humans. They lived serene, simple, uncomplicated lives that had not changed much in thousands of years.

Roberts lived with the Karran people for three months, observing their ways, making notes.

He was accepted. They found his height amusing, his pale skin a source of fascination. They found his camera and torch novel at first, then soon lost interest.

He befriended an old man – old, that is, by the reckoning of the Karran people: he was in his early forties – called M'dendo. They sat outside Roberts' tent as the rapid jungle twilight descended, smoking gourd pipes of some noxious green leaf. Over the course of the months, M'dendo told Roberts about his life and the history of his people.

They were watched over by the gods of the jungle, M'dendo said. When they died, they entered the spirit world, along with every other creature on Earth. The Karran people knew nothing of the outside world, nor were they interested.

They had seen one other white man before – the geologist from the university – many years ago.

"Before that," M'dendo told Roberts, "the Oth had visited."

"The Oth?" Roberts asked.

"Small people. Even smaller than us. This high," M'dendo said, holding his hand a metre from the packed earth of the clearing.

"Where did these people come from?"

M'dendo gestured. "Outside," he said, and changed the subject.

Roberts assumed the story referred to beings of the Karran's spirit world, and soon forgot about the Oth.

Later, back in New York, he wrote up his findings and published a paper in the *Anthropological Review* titled, "Birth and Rebirth: the ontological belief system of the Karran people."

Five years later Roberts returned to upper Congo and the Karran people.

HIS FRIEND M'DENDO WAS dead – gone to join his ancestors in the spirit world. Roberts felt a deep sadness, even though he had not expected to find the old man still living.

One evening, as twilight closed over the jungle like a lid, Roberts sat outside his tent and made notes by torchlight. A broad-faced woman with tribal scarification upon her cheeks came and sat beside him. She was Lana, the daughter of M'dendo.

They talked.

Roberts recalled something that M'dendo had told him. "Lana, the last time I was here I spoke to your father. He told me of the Oth."

"Yes, the Oth. He told me of these people too. They came many, many years ago, before I was born. They stayed with my people, watching us. My father spoke with the Oth."

"What did they tell him?"

"The Oth told him about the world outside, the place from which they came."

Roberts smiled to himself. Was the name 'Oth' the Karran word for the representatives of loggers, he wondered, or prospectors? Corporations often used native peoples as emissaries in order to gain the jungle-dwellers' trust. But

M'dendo had said that the Oth were even *smaller* than the Karran.

He asked Lana if the Oth were Africans.

"No, no. They were not Africans. They were not my colour."

"Then what colour were they?"

She pulled an expressive frown. She looked into his tent, reached inside and took out his torch. She fumbled for the button and pressed it, then played the light across the ground.

"They were this colour," she said, indicating the conical beam of white light.

So the Oth were smaller than the Karran people and the colour of light.

Roberts asked her more about the Oth, but Lana could tell him nothing.

He asked other members of the tribe, and one old man, Manka, told him that in three years from now the Oth would return. "You see, they come back every fifty years and watch us. Three years from now, at the third full moon of the year, the Oth will return."

He pressed Manka for details, but the old man was unable, or unwilling, to tell him more.

Roberts returned home and wrote up his notes in a paper published as "Rites and Rituals: Ancestor worship among the Karran People."

And he made arrangements to return to Africa in three years' time.

ROBERTS SAT OUTSIDE HIS TENT in the silver light of the full moon.

He sensed anticipation among the Karran people, and asked Lana about the visitation of the Oth. She shook her head, saying only that they would come in their own time.

The full moon came and went, and Roberts resigned himself to disappointment.

Then one evening, unable to sleep, he sat outside his tent and gazed across the clearing. As the moon waned and Roberts thought about taking his leave within the week, he caught a glimpse of a white shape on the edge of the jungle.

He held his breath. The jungle was silent. The Karran people were in their huts, sleeping.

He stared at the white figure as it approached. Then he saw others, a dozen of the supernal, glowing figures, converging on the clearing in absolute silence. He stared in wonder and not a little apprehension, his heart hammering.

The first figure crossed the clearing and halted before him, while its fellows hung back, watching.

Roberts smiled, then laughed – a little hysterically, he later admitted – as he stared at the creature.

It was a metre high, and glowing white as if illuminated from within, with a thin face and large black, staring eyes. It possessed no nose to speak of and no ears that Roberts could see.

He said, "Who are you?"

To his amazement, the creature replied in his own language, "We are the Oth."

"From…?" His voice caught. He tried again, "Where are you from?" though he knew full well what the answer would be.

The being lifted a stick-thin fingers and pointed. Through a rent in the jungle canopy Roberts made out the constellation of Lyra.

"You call our star Vega," said the being.

"And… and what are you doing here?"

The creature replied, "What are you doing here, Dr Roberts?" And Roberts gasped, for he had not told the alien his name.

The creature retreated, joined its fellows, and moved off into the jungle.

Over the course of the next week the creatures would appear from nowhere and trail the Karran people – who tolerated the Oth's presence with amused smiles, but never spoke to the visitors. Again and again Roberts followed the aliens and asked questions. They deigned not to reply.

Then one evening as he sat outside his tent writing of his amazing discovery, a member of the Oth approached him. It might have been the same one which had spoken to him a week earlier, but he had no way of telling them apart.

"We are leaving," it said.

"And you will return, in fifty years?"

"We will return then, yes."

"I… I would like to speak with you for longer. I have questions…" He laughed. He had a thousand questions, a lifetime of questions waiting to be asked!

"We are leaving soon," said the creature.

"Tell me," Roberts said, "why you have not contacted… *my* people; the governments of my people, the powerful?"

The being's gesture took in the clearing, the rude huts, the people sleeping peacefully within. "Because," it said at last, "these people tell us everything we need to know about the virtues of *Homo sapiens.*"

ROBERTS RETURNED TO NEW YORK and began a paper titled "Between the Object and the Subject: the role of the Extraterrestrial Watcher in the history of the Karran people", but never completed it.

He considered what he had discovered deep in the Congo jungle, and came to a decision. He destroyed his half-finished paper, his notes and the photographs he had taken of the Oth, made his farewells and left America.

He returned to Africa and lived the rest of his life with the Karran people, who viewed his presence with tolerant amusement. He soon adapted to their way of life, and considered his old existence in the West with the wisdom of an old man who looks back upon a wayward childhood.

In fifty years he would be almost eighty-five: he anticipated his second meeting with the Oth.

TAKEAWAY

TONY BALLANTYNE

STEPHANIE STRETCHED THE PHONE CORD to its full extent and leant around the doorway, gazing into the tiny kitchen beyond.

"There's a customer on the phone wanting two sweet and sour porks delivered."

Mr Ho shook fried rice from his wok, expertly filling a silver container.

"Why you telling me that, Stephanie? Can't you see I'm busy?"

"I know, Mr Ho, but the customer wants the order delivered to the anthill on Stonebreak Lane."

Mr Ho frowned. "Ah, that is unusual. Ants usually prefer Lemon Chicken. Tell them ten minutes."

Stephanie looked at Mr Ho. It wasn't like him to make jokes. It wasn't like him to do anything except to cook and to chastise her for not working hard enough.

"Are you winding me up, Mr Ho?"

"No, Stephanie."

Stephanie held his gaze for a moment, then she shrugged.

"Ten minutes," she said into the phone, and put it down.

Mr Ho began to lecture her.

"Your trouble, Stephanie, is you lazy. Think too much about boys and not enough about work. Tell me, you learn speak French at school?"

Stephanie came into the kitchen and leant on the counter as Mr Ho rinsed the black wok under the tap. Steam hissed up.

"Learn French?" said Stephanie. "Why should I when I can run transl-8 or Lebab or Syntactix? Who learns languages nowadays?"

The wok was already back on the flame.

"Wise people. Look at me. I come to England, I learn to speak the language properly. I don't use computer or headset everyday. I want to be treated as Englishman, not foreigner."

"I don't see what that's got to do with the ants."

"How you think they speak English?" Mr Ho dropped a handful of onions and pork into the wok. "You think ants learn for themselves?"

"No. But I didn't think ants could use computers."

"Of course they can't. But software is context sensitive. If you learned languages, you would understand. Words aren't enough, need context too. Like when you say to me 'nice shirt, Mr Ho,' the other day. You being sarcastic girl, think I not realise."

"No I wasn't…"

"You think I not clever because I speak with accent. But translating software know about accent and everything else.

Context is everything. And context get bigger and bigger. Not just tone of voice, but facial expression, set of body, the whole environment. What called the frame. And so translating software need to do more than just listen to voice, but also to read body language and look at whole environment. Ants part of environment. Small wonder software start to translate language for them, too."

"But why are ants ordering Chinese food?"

"Because my food very tasty. I good cook. Very popular take away. You think they want to eat Mr Mahmood's horrible curry? Rancid ghee and chilli powder."

"No! You know that's not what I mean! Why aren't they out hunting for leaves or whatever it is ants eat?"

"Why don't you go out and hunt or farm for food? Takeaway is easier. And tastier. And more efficient for ants. Nest is thriving. Is now one hundred yards across!"

"What? How come I didn't know about that?"

"You lazy girl. Only think about boys. Ants nest on television, you not see?"

"No! But…where do they get the money from?"

"Ant nest is near computer assembly factory. Ants ideal for manipulating small parts. Cheaper than machinery too. Ants don't ask much money. Only get enough to buy tasty Chinese food."

"That's ridiculous!"

"No it's not. Is animals adapting to new eco-system. You not listen to biology either? Too busy speaking to boyfriend."

Mr Ho dropped a handful of pineapple and pepper into the wok. He shook it in a rattle of steam and hissing of frying.

Stephanie bit her lip. "Are all the animals ordering takeaways, then?"

"No. Most animals lazy. Won't move with times. Like relatives who stay at home and not grasp opportunities of western world."

Mr Ho picked up a ladle and, tossing the contents of the pan all the while, spooned three lots of red sauce over the ingredients.

"You're winding me up, right?" said Stephanie. "You're seriously telling me that because translation software looks at the whole context of language, it has enabled communication between species, the results of which are that whole eco-systems are changing due to animals exploiting new opportunities. The result of this is that an ant's nest is now ordering takeaway food bought using money it earned by working in a microprocessor plant, this being a more viable means of existence?"

"Elegantly put. See? You clever girl when you want to be."

"So why does that mean I should learn French?"

"Ants not know language properly, not know wider context, so just respond to need. Get exploited. All that work in computer plant, and only get paid enough to buy takeaway."

The sweet and sour pork was ready. Mr Ho expertly divided the contents of the wok between two silver trays.

"All done," he said. "Feed hungry ants. Very good customers. Ah! Here come delivery girl!"

"Delivery *girl?*" said Stephanie. "What happened to Adam?"

"Too expensive. And lazy. Prefer spend time chatting to you than delivering tasty food. Delilah more reliable.

Stephanie looked down at Delilah as she trotted into the little kitchen, tail wagging. She was very good, eyes to the front, not stopping to sniff anything. Mr Ho bagged the order, putting the handle into her mouth.

"Good girl," he said as the dog trotted out of the shop. "Work very hard."

Stephanie watched her go.

The next day, she signed up for French lessons.

THE HISTORY OF EARTH

ERIC BROWN

IT WAS THE YEAR seven billion, one hundred million – give or take a few hundred thousand years. Not that anyone was counting.

I lived alone in a manse on the edge of the Equatorial Meadows and spent my time reading the many texts of the past and foraging for relics of times long gone.

And writing.

When I was not working, I sat on the verandah and stared out at the sun, swollen now so that it filled half the heavens.

I was reading the Lavat, the holy book of a people who lived in the Fourth Cycle of planet Earth, some forty-five million years – give or take – after the first intelligent *Homo sapiens* walked the planet.

The book was nonsense, of course, like all the other supposedly holy books that came before and after it; but it had provided its disciples with a *modus operandi*, at the time.

I finished the Lavat and moved on, studied the many written histories of the people extant at that time; and then I studied the people who followed these people, who called themselves the Kahl – super-humanoid beings, part-human, part-alien, whose reign on planet Earth lasted longer than any other, some thirty-five million years.

They passed, of course, as did every race.

I wrote of the Kahl, and their successors, the Passand'ar, and their successors, the Rho…

For three thousand years I wrote of Earth's twilight, the time before every sentient being left the planet to explore the vastness of the universe.

And then my work was finished.

I sat on the verandah and watched the sun rise and set.

THEN ONE DAY THE KLK'JA landed their ship of light on the Equatorial Meadows before my manse.

They approached in a crowd of thirty-three, as they had done many times before.

They spoke as one, these beings of light.

"Have you finished, Creature?"

"I have finished."

"Truly? We have been coming here every year for twenty-five thousand years, and always your reply is the same: 'I have not yet finished'. But now…"

"But now," I said, "I have."

The klk'ja – whose name translates as Librarians – turned to each other and twittered in their own language.

"Then, with respect, may we take the finished work?"

I inclined my head. "You may."

And I passed the leading klk'ja the pin on which the Work was stored.

They paused, and all thirty-three stared at me.

At last they spoke, "What are you, Creature, that you sit here year after year, and range far and wide across your deserted world, exploring and foraging, and always coming back to write your eternal history?"

I laughed, "Not eternal," I said. "For now it is finished."

"But what kind of creature are you?" the klk'ja asked again.

I contemplated the words. I had often wondered this myself.

At last I said, "I was constructed over three billion, four hundred million years ago by a race of Fabricators known as the Hleth," I said. "They wanted to make a being that would last, that would outlive themselves, a being whose sole function and duty was to record. I am their child, if you will."

The klk'ja repeated the word amongst themselves.

"Are you not sad?"

"In what way?" I asked.

"Sad, first, that you are alone, that there are no more of your kind?"

I contemplated the question, and reflected, and at last I replied, "No, for that is why I was built. To be alone. To investigate. To record."

The supernal beings of light inclined their headpieces as one. "That we understand," they said. "Second, are you not sad... now that your work is done?"

I smiled at this.

"No, I am not sad, for I was created in order to write a history of the planet Earth, from its very creation to the present day, and this I have succeeded in accomplishing. I am not sad. I am joyous. I have fulfilled all my makers' desires."

A silence settled over the gathering, and the sun set slowly behind their crystal ship, and the long evening of planet Earth continued.

They said, "And what will you do now, Creature?"

"Now…?" I sat and stared at the sunset. "Now I will write no more, and explore no more, and surmise no more. I will sit and contemplate the sun, and I will speak with any beings who should pass along this way."

"Creature," said the klk'ja, every one of them bending in a way I interpreted as a gesture of gratitude, "we thank you for the History, and say farewell."

"Farewell," I said.

They moved *en masse* back to their ship, carrying with them – bearing aloft – the pin containing the History of my planet, the story of everything that ever happened upon the face of the world; every work of fiction I could find, which I absorbed and re-interpreted, every factual account, every record of every movement of every being which ever walked upon the planet – this thanks to the reality-simulators created by the Vilk, who lived three million years ago – a record of every science and every fable and *everything* that had ever existed on my planet.

My gift, the Fabricator's gift, to the universe.

I was, after all, over three billion years old.

The klk'ja's ship took-off and disappeared into the heavens. I watched the sun sink over the horizon and the stars come out in their immensity across the face of the universe, and I thanked my makers, once again.

It was the year seven billion, one hundred million – give or take a few hundred thousand years. Not that anyone was counting.

TONY BALLANTYNE AND MR BROWN

TONY BALLANTYNE

2013

"ENTER!"

Eric was sitting in his leather armchair in the middle of the library, volume 4 of *The Complete Rupert Croft-Cooke* open in his lap. I stood respectfully, waiting for him to finish a paragraph. Eventually, he placed a finger upon his place on the page and looked at me over his half moon spectacles.

"Tony, Tony, Tony," he said. "What have brought for me today?"

I hurried forward, holding up the black rectangle I held in my hand.

"I've brought you this! It's an ebook reader."

I thrust the device towards him. He took it between thumb and forefinger, as a vegetarian might hold a steak.

"And an ebook reader is…?" he said.

"You store books on it!" I replied. "Download them from the internet. You can store thousands of books at once, carry a library around in your pocket!"

I had let my enthusiasm carry me away. Eric waited for me to calm down.

"Tony, Tony, Tony," he said, and I knew that I'd done the wrong thing in bringing this machine to his library.

"This," he said, handing back the ebook, "is just a collection of words. This…" he held up the complete Croft-Cooke "is a book! It is more than just words. It has weight! Feel it! Smell it! There is something about a physical object that transcends words themselves. Look over there…"

He pointed to his collection of Ace Doubles, tracked down over long years in SF conventions, souks and bazaars around the world, now lovingly rebound in gold inlaid calfskin.

"Could this 'e-book'," he made air bunnies with his fingers, "replace those? Hmm?"

"Well, to be honest, you could download the complete collection in about five minutes…"

"The conversation is over! I have work to do!"

He picked up his glass of port and resumed reading. The audience was at an end.

1474

"Enter!"

Eric was sitting in his wooden chair in the middle of the library, a hand illuminated volume of the New Testament in his lap. I stood respectfully, waiting for him to finish a verse. Eventually, he placed a finger upon his place on the page and looked at me over his half moon spectacles.

"Tony, Tony, Tony," he said. "What have brought for me today?"

I hurried forward, holding up the black rectangle I held in my hand.

"I've brought you this! It's a book, printed from Mr Caxton's most excellent press!"

I thrust a book towards him. He took it between thumb and forefinger, as a vegetarian might hold a steak.

"Recuyell of the Historyes of Troye" he read.

"It's a translation of a French courtly romance written by Raoul Lefevre, chaplain to Philip III, Duke of Burgundy. It's the first book to be printed in the English language!"

I had let my enthusiasm carry me away. Eric waited for me to calm down.

"Tony, Tony, Tony," he said, and I knew that I'd done the wrong thing in bringing this soulless tome to his library.

"This," he said, handing back the book, "is just a collection of words. This…" he held up the bible "is a book! The letters on this page were not simply stamped there by some press! They were written by hand, each letter invested with individual care and attention, each unique in its own right! The idea that one can reduce thoughts to nothing more than twenty six identical letters is clearly preposterous!"

"Well, to be honest, that's all the alphabet really is…"

"The conversation is over! I have work to do!"

He picked up his glass of wine and resumed reading. The audience was at an end.

354

"ENTER!"

Eric was sitting in his wooden stool in the middle of the hall, a scroll on his lap. I stood respectfully, waiting for him to finish a verse. Eventually, he placed a finger upon his place on the page and looked at me.

"Tony, Tony, Tony," he said. "What have brought for me today?"

I hurried forward, holding up the black rectangle I held in my hand.

"I've brought you this! It's a codex! A collection of scrolls bound together in a more portable fashion. You can carry this with you easily as you travel the country, preaching the word of the Lord."

I thrust the codex towards him. He took it between thumb and forefinger, as a vegetarian might hold a steak.

"The Gospel according to Matthew," he read.

"And Mark! And Luke! And John! All in one volume! And there's pictures, too!"

I had let my enthusiasm carry me away. Eric waited for me to calm down.

"Tony, Tony, Tony," he said, and I knew that I'd done the wrong thing in bringing this soulless tome before him.

"This," he said, handing back the codex, "is just a collection of words. This…" he held up the scroll "is a scroll! It's rounder and more curly! You can open it top and bottom. If you let it go at one end it goes *whup whup whup* as it wraps itself up. Can your *codex*" – he made airbunnies with his fingers – "close itself?"

"Yes, but scrolls can get squashed quite easily…"

"The conversation is over! I have work to do!"

He picked up his glass of mead and resumed reading. The audience was at an end.

A long time ago
"ENTER!"

Eric was sitting on a step in the temple, staring upwards in contemplation. I waited for his eyes to focus upon me.

"Tony, Tony, Tony," he said. "What have brought for me today?"

I hurried forward, holding up the roll of papyrus I held in my hand.

"I've brought you this! It's a scroll!"

I thrust the papyrus towards him. He took it between thumb and forefinger, as a vegetarian might hold a steak.

"Those are words!" I said, showing the patterns written on the paper. "They tell a story!"

I had let my enthusiasm carry me away. Eric waited for me to calm down.

"Tony, Tony, Tony," he said, and I knew that I'd done the wrong thing in bringing this soulless piece of papyrus to him.

"This," he said, tapping his head, "is a brain. It contains thoughts passed on by *Oral Tradition*. Thoughts that are regularly examined and improved upon before being passed to others through the medium of speech. This…" He pointed to the scroll "…is sterile and lifeless! Like a fly trapped in amber, it contains the form, but it does not contain the spark, the essence, the vitality…"

"Oh."

"The conversation is over! I have work to do!"

He picked up his bladder of goat's milk and resumed thinking. The audience was at an end.

Even longer ago

"HEY ERIC! I JUST HEARD a great story!"

"A story? What's that?"

"Oh. Never mind."

MEMORIAL

ERIC BROWN

I THOUGHT HE WAS A reporter, come to interview me about the Second World War. I've had a procession of them through the cottage recently, wanting my story, and I thought he was just another one.

Well, my hearing's not so good these days – what do you expect? I'm 104 next week – and my eyesight's not the best either. But my memory is just as sharp as it always was, and I suppose that's what matters.

He rang first, to see if he could have an interview. Although I only heard half of what he said, I said yes.

Lest we forget, they say. Never a truer word spoken!

He arrived at the cottage in a dapper suit: tall, distinguished, in his fifties. He didn't look like a reporter, but I never twigged. "Charles Gayle," he said, "From…" I didn't catch the name of his paper.

I sat him in the garden and made him a cup of tea. It was a wonderful day, the sun bright, birds singing… He asked me about my experiences of the Second World War. I started by telling him how I'd lied about my age.

"I was fourteen when I joined up, but I looked older. I'd borrowed my older brother's birth certificate, you see. They hardly gave it a glance, though. Then it was up to Catterick and basic training before you could say Jack Robinson. Mum was upset, but Dad said let him be. I think he was proud I was doing what he hadn't been able to do in the Great War, on account of his bad leg."

Gayle asked about my first battle experience, and I paused a while before telling him.

I'd spoken to very few people about what happened at Arnhem – what I saw, and what I did. I told my wife, because that's the kind of thing you tell your wife, but I kept silent when my son and daughter asked the inevitable questions. Why confront them with the horror of warfare, before they could find out for themselves?

"The day after parachuting into Holland," I said, "I saw my best friend take a round in the torso. Danny Shaw from Bolton, he was. A gentle lad, all smiles. He fell next to me; that is, his head and shoulders hit the ground. And... and I don't know why I did it... but I reached out and touched his cheek, just like that, and I wept."

I took a gulp of tea. Danny's a long time dead now, but I haven't forgotten him. How can you forget something like that?

"And then, a few days later, it was my turn to kill."

Gayle asked, quietly, "What happened?"

"We'd advanced on a farmhouse and taken it. There were still a few Germans in one of the outbuildings, so we lobbed in a grenade. And when one lad jumped through a side window, clutching his spilled guts in his hands, I... Well, I like to think I put him out of his misery, but the truth was that I'd have shot him anyway. I look back and I'm not proud of what I did, then or later... But at the time I was fighting for king and country, and it was duty...kill or be killed... them or us...all the old words to make the unacceptable acceptable. Same old story, and it's still going on."

I fell silent, and closed my eyes.

"Korea," I said, "Vietnam, the Falklands, Kuwait, Iraq, Afghanistan...and where is it now? Never mind, it'll come to me."

"Nigeria," Gayle said.

"And young lads and lasses are still joining up, still fighting for king and country."

"Would you like to do something," he said suddenly, "to make people think again?"

I laughed. "Think again? But it's all in here!" I thumped my chest. "We're still animals. Still savages!"

"Even so, if something could be done to remind people of the savagery of war..."

"Cloud Cuckoo Land. There's nothing we could do."

He stared at me, calculation in his eyes. "There something that you, personally, could do."

I laughed. "And what's that?"

"Did you realise," he said, "that you're the last?"

"The last? The last what?"

"The very last surviving combatant of World War Two."

That was what all the reporters had told me, what all the ballyhoo was about…

The last.

I just shook my head, and thought about it, and a great sadness came over me.

And he told me who he was – and what I could do, or rather what he and his company could do, to help people remember.

Lest we forget…

Then he said goodbye, asked me to consider his offer, and left

I sat in the sunlight and considered his words. And I wondered, not for the first time, Why me? Why me, from the hundreds of thousands, the millions, who fought in World War Two?

Gayle wasn't a reporter. He represented a company called OmegaGen and they were in the final stages of developing a range of drugs that would not only halt the ageing process but restore health to ailing individuals.

And they would be honoured, he'd told me, if I would consent to be the first human being on which the drugs were used.

"You would enjoy another hundred years of active life."

I would be a relic, of course, a living memorial. I would be known only for being the last surviving soldier from an old and almost forgotten war.

I'd lived with the acceptance of death for so long that it was frightening to consider the alternative. I'd lived, also, with a deep mistrust of all governments and organisations.

And as for companies promising longevity...

He'd left me his phone number, and asked me to ring when I'd made my decision.

I sat in the sunlight, listening to the birdsong, thinking through what Gayle had said, and considering the future.

BROUGHT TO EARTH

TONY BALLANTYNE

"ARE YOU REALLY AN astronaut, mister?"

"I am. At least, I was."

The boy was about ten years old, I guessed. Another resident of Chiltern House, judging by the cheap coat over his kameez, the rough north-western accent. Dark hair and blue eyes.

"Where did you go?"

"Venus. Mars. Once I made it to Neptune."

For a moment, for the briefest moment, a look of admiration crossed the boy's face. It was quickly replaced by something else.

"Bastard!" he said. "Wasteful bastard." And then he spat at me, turned and ran back down the long concrete hallway.

I RODE THE LIFT TO the eighteenth floor of Chiltern house and knocked on Mia's door. I got a great view across the rainswept extent of the Pennines from up there.

Mia opened the door to the flat. She looked awful. Way too thin, with sunken cheeks and dark shadows under her eyes. She'd shaved her head all the time I'd worked with her, but now her hair hung long and lank and greasy around her pale face.

"You look good," I lied, kissing her on the cheek.

"No, I don't," said Mia. "You're not looking bad though, Gil."

It was true. I had my daughter to look after me, to help me out with a little money at the end of the month, to invite me to dinner once a week.

"Come in."

She led me through a narrow hallway into a tiny lounge/diner. The window gave a view north over Rochdale, it showed the broken down tower blocks and tired houses.

"I've saved this for us," said Mia, bringing out a half bottle of cheap whiskey. "A little celebration."

"Oh! And I brought you this!"

I handed across the package. Mia looked at in wonder.

"Steak! Real steak! I can't!"

"Yes, you can. My daughter's the manager of a supermarket. She earns a good wage. Take it!"

"I'll cook it now. We can share it."

"No, it's a treat for you."

"I insist."

She pulled a frying pan from a little cupboard. The base was so thin the steak would burn if she tried to sear it properly, but what could you do? I found two glasses and poured the whisky.

"Cheers!" said Mia, clinking glasses.

She poured a little oil in the pan, set it heating.

"So," she said. "How long has it been since you came down to Earth?"

"Three years."

"What have you been up to since then?"

"Nothing much. Keeping my head down. Travelling around, trying to keep in touch with old crew."

She dropped the steaks in the pan. Too soon, it wasn't hot enough. I guess she wasn't used to cooking real meat.

"What are they up to?"

What do you think? I wanted to say. *The same as you and me. Walking without going anywhere. Staring at the night sky, lifted on tiptoes when the stars are out. Just existing, now that they cut our wings.*

"Alison is doing okay for herself. Got a job on a cruise liner. Sailing all over the world."

"That's a good job for an ex-spacer," said Mia, though I could hear the faint edge in her voice. It would always be second best…

"Bikram is living with his brother's family. Working in the family restaurant. And Jean… Jean's doing okay."

"And the rest…?"

"Well, you know."

She knew. We both knew. You could spot people like us from across a room. People who had fallen to earth. People whose early promise had sent them to the top before gravity had pulled them down.

She turned the steaks. She stared at them, not looking at me.

"I heard that Sean was beaten to death."

"He was." I stared at her thin, bony hands. "He was mouthing off in a pub in Rotherham. Saying how we should be spending money on rockets, we should be looking outwards to the universe, looking for a better tomorrow rather than staying at home and fighting another war. He picked the wrong crowd. There's a big arms factory in Rotherham. Lot of jobs there. They didn't want a starsailor telling them they shouldn't be in work…"

She nodded. She'd had a thing with Sean, I knew. The pair of them had flown transport to the Belt several times. Eighteen months together, just the two of them and a hold full of machinery. Relationships could be pretty intense.

"What do the people here think of your past?" I asked, waving my arm, indicating the rest of the block of flats.

"They don't know. I intend to keep it that way."

"Probably the right choice."

She served up the steaks. We sat and ate them. We didn't have a lot to say. We'd used up our conversation in the best part of our lives, floating between the stars.

"Did we do the right thing?" she asked. "All that money spent in space, and there were people starving here on Earth. You could see their point."

"What do you think?" I asked. "They stopped the space program and there are *still* people starving."

She wiped a finger on her plate, licked the bloody juices from it.

"I think there's some bread to mop up with," she said, rising from her seat.

"That'll be nice," I said. I built my life from little pleasures now.

THE ALIEN TITHE

ERIC BROWN

ON THE DAY ALLOTTED TO me, I left Starship City with my sons and daughters and trekked through the mountains to the high dome of the aliens.

The first night we camped beneath the massed stars of the galactic core. We built a fire and ate roasted vegetables grown on our own land. Nightbirds boomed from a nearby grove of luminescent trees. After the meal we lay back and took in the beauty of the view. Fifty kilometres away, spanning a pass between two towering peaks, the aliens' dome reflected the starlight like a mounted gem.

WE SET OFF AT SUNRISE and took the path that climbed the ravine, soon leaving the forest in our wake. In three days we would arrive at the dome, and be received.

Harry: "I'm excited!"

Olivia: "Me too."

Paul: "A new life awaits us!"

Emma: "I'll miss our... our old life." Emma, the quiet, thoughtful one; Emma the compassionate.

ON THE THIRD DAY WE reached the first pass. This was where my children would look back for the last time and see the plain where they had grown up, and the Starship that had given them life.

We paused as one and stared down the mountainside. The silver length of the Starship, broken-backed, sprawled across the plain where twenty-five years ago it had crash-landed. Around it, radiating on roads like spokes, was the city which was my home.

Harry: "Goodbye Starship City."

Olivia: "Goodbye old life."

Paul: "Hello new life!"

Emma: "I'll miss you, Starship City."

We turned and climbed, and five minutes later I looked over my shoulder. A jutting outcrop of rock hid the city from view.

THAT NIGHT, AS WE SAT cross-legged around the camp-fire, I told my children the Landfall Story.

"It should have been an easy landing," I said, "but there was a problem with the ship's smartcore. A communication glitch between the 'core and the propulsion system. We came down too fast. It was a miracle we landed in one piece – or rather in two pieces."

My children stared at me with wide eyes. Harry: "And what then?"

"Mum and me, we came round from suspension to find the ship burning. We and others put out the fire, assessed the damage, counted the dead. Out of five thousand colonists, over two thousand had perished. Also, many of us were injured, badly injured. And the ship's medical chamber was destroyed..."

Olivia: "And then the aliens came..."

Paul: "And helped us."

Emma, "And asked for something in return."

I was silent for a time, staring up at the pulsing stars of the core.

"They healed our wounded, nursed the sick. Without the aliens..."

Harry: "Many colonists would have died."

Olivia: "The colony would have failed."

Paul: "We would not be here."

Emma: "But the aliens came to our rescue and demanded... tithe."

The coals glowed. I stared around at the bright faces of my children. "They demanded compensation for helping us, and stated the price for allowing us to remain on their planet. We had, after all, come here uninvited."

The fire dwindled and we slept.

WE WERE ONE DAY AWAY from the dome.

Its crystal beauty dominated the mountain landscape ahead, scintillating in Antares' ruddy light. The dome's surface was opaque, its interior mysteries hidden from sight. We climbed above the tree-line and the temperature dropped. We donned protective clothing, and that evening built a bigger fire and sat closer to its dancing flames.

Harry: "Tell us about Earth again."

Olivia: "Why did humankind leave?"

Paul: "What did you and mum do on Earth?"

Emma: "And were you happier there, or here?"

I leaned forward, towards the warmth of the fire. "Earth was... exhausted," I said. "Depleted. We had ruined it, taken everything, given back nothing. We had to leave in order to... to grow, to learn... to survive." I smiled at each of my children in turn. "Your mother and I were ecologists back on Earth – farmers, just as we are now. And..." I looked at Emma. "And we are happier here," I said.

WE SLOWED AS WE APPROACHED the pass, and the alien dome that straddled its span. Only now, a kilometre from its great curving opalescent walls, did we apprehend its true dimensions. It must have been five kilometres across, and at least two high. At ground level, a dozen arched portals gave access to its enigmatic interior.

We walked slowly, like pilgrims, towards our destination.

We paused before the portal which reared to the height of ten men above us. At our approach, its surface deopaqued and we beheld a bare, white atrium within.

A being emerged: humanoid but perilously thin, almost insect-like. It regarded me, and then my children, with vast faceted eyes.

"Come," it said, gesturing inside with a stick-thin arm.

I hugged Harry and Olivia and Paul. "Goodbye," I said. They were bright-eyed, eager to experience the next stage of their young lives.

I hugged Emma to me and she whispered, "Why, daddy? What do they want with us?"

I stared into her eyes and told her the truth. "I don't know, honey. I don't know."

She smiled at me one last time, then turned and joined the others as they followed the alien through the portal. At its threshold they turned and waved, and I lifted a hand in return.

Then the entrance opaqued and my children were lost to sight.

Frozen, I turned and made the long trek home.

When I came to the first pass I looked down at the city sprawling beneath me, at the thousand homesteads and the colonists working the land.

Each family with five children, each family harbouring its own weight of gratitude and sadness.

SHAMIRA WAS WAITING FOR ME when I returned, Shamira who this time had been unable to bring herself to accompany us. She had remained on the farm, harvesting the crops with the help of our biological daughter.

I watched them as they worked side by side, and tears came to my eyes.

The following day Shamira and I made the journey to the starship and donated our gift of genetic material to the

Processor, the artificial womb to be used – the mission planners had said, all those years ago – in case of emergencies.

The official told us that in six months our children, two girls and two boys, would come to term, and we could take delivery of them.

And ten years after that I would make the pilgrimage to the alien dome to discharge our obligation.

Then the official asked if we would care to register our children's names.

We thought a while, and then spoke.

"Harry," I said.

"Olivia," Shamira said.

"Paul."

"Emma."

That night I stood at the door of my daughter's bedroom and stared at her as she slept, and considered what Emma had asked me. *"And were you happier there, or here?"*

I closed the door quietly and made my way to bed.

IF ONLY…

TONY BALLANTYNE

"DOCTOR," SAID SACHA, "CAN YOU give me your assurance that this injection won't harm my children?"

"Well, there is always some risk, Ms Melham. I do have a leaflet that explains everything…"

Sacha placed a finger on the table.

"I don't need a leaflet, Doctor. I simply want your assurance that this injection will cause Willow and Gregory no harm…"

Doctor James Ferriday gazed at the finger.

"As I said, there is always a small risk, but if you look you will see that this is less than the possibility of…"

Sacha held up her hand.

"Please, Doctor. Don't try and confuse the issue."

"I'm not trying to confuse the issue, I'm simply presenting you with the facts…"

Sacha rose to her feet.

"Well, I think I've heard enough. Willow, Gregory, put your coats back on. Thank you, Doctor, we'll be… what's that?"

James's screen flashed red and green.

"Oh dear," he said, reading the yellow writing scrolling across the monitor. "I think you should take a seat."

Sacha did so. Her son slipped his hand into hers.

"What's the matter, mummy?"

"Nothing, dear. Is everything okay, Doctor?"

"I'm sorry, Ms Melham…" he began, and then more kindly, "I'm sorry, Sacha, but you've crossed the threshold. I'm afraid to say, you're not allowed science anymore."

"I'm what?"

"You're not allowed science anymore," repeated James.

Sacha's lips moved as she tried to process what he had said.

"You're saying that you're refusing my children treatment?"

"No," said James. "Quite the opposite. You and your children will always be entitled to the best of medical care. It's just that you, Sacha, no longer have a say in it. I shall administer the vaccination immediately."

"What?" Sacha sat up, eyes burning with indignation. "How dare you? I, and my husband, are the only ones that say how my family is run."

"Well, yes," said James. "But you no longer have a say in things where science is involved. You're not allowed science anymore."

"I never heard anything so ridiculous! Who decided that?"

"The universe."

"The universe? Why should the universe say I'm not allowed science anymore?"

"Because you haven't paid science enough attention. You've had the opportunity to read the facts and the education to be able to analyse them, yet you have consistently chosen not to."

"The education?" exclaimed Sacha. "Hah! My science education was terrible. None of my teachers could explain anything properly."

"Really?" said James, "that would certainly be cause for appeal..."

He pressed a couple of buttons. Tables of figures appeared on the screen.

"No," he said, shaking his head. "I'm sorry... it turns out that your teachers were all really rather excellent. You went to a very good public school, after all. If you look at your teachers' results you will see they added significant value to their pupils' attainment."

Sacha pouted.

"Well, they didn't like me."

"Possibly..."

He pressed a couple more buttons.

"What?" said Sacha, hearing his sharp intake of breath.

"Look at this," said James, scrolling down a long table. "Times and dates of occasions when you've proudly admitted to not being good at maths."

"What's the matter with that? I'm not."

"It's not the lack of ability, Sacha, it's the fact that you're proud of it. You'd never be proud of being illiterate. Why do you think your innumeracy is a cause for celebration?"

"Because… Well…."

"That's why you're not allowed science anymore."

"This is outrageous!" snarled Sacha. "How can this happen?"

"Oh, that's easy," said James. "Magic."

"Magic?" said Sacha, her eyes suddenly shining. "You mean there's really such a thing?"

"Of course not. But I can't explain to you how it's really done because you're not allowed science anymore."

Sacha fumbled for her handbag.

"I'm calling the BBC," she said. "I'm a producer there, you know. I'll report you."

"Report me to who you like," said James. "The story will never get out. All your cameras and microphones and things work on science."

Sacha gazed at him.

"Who gave you the right to control my life?"

"You've got it the wrong way round. *You* gave the right to control your life *away*. You're the one who chose to ignore the way the world works."

"Hah!" said Sacha. "The way the world works! Bloody scientists. You think the world is all numbers and machines and levers. You don't understand anything about the soul or spirit."

"Of course I do," said James. "I've been happily married for twenty years. I have two children that I love. I play the piano, I enjoy reading. It's just that I have additional ways of looking at things."

Sacha stood up.

"Willow, Gregory. We're going home," she glared at James. "That is if I'm still allowed to drive? You don't have something against women drivers as well do you, Doctor?"

"This is nothing to do with you being female, Ms Melham," said James, calmly. "This is purely about your attitude to science. Now, before you go, I'll administer the injection to the three of you."

"You will not! I will not allow it."

"I told you, you have no choice."

"Why? Because I disagree with you?"

For this first time, James's anger showed itself.

"No!" he snapped. "You don't get it! You're *allowed* to disagree with me, I *want* you to disagree with me! I'd *love* to engage in reasoned debate with you. But until you take the trouble to understand what you're talking about, you're not allowed science anymore. Now, roll up your sleeve."

Sacha muttered something under her breath.

"What's in the injection?" said James. "You know, you start asking questions like that, you might get science back…"

VISITING PLANET EARTH

ERIC BROWN

I VISIT YOUR PLANET FROM time to time, but it really is too painful.

My race is immortal now, and our client races are immortal, too, or have transcended bodily form and exist in virtual realms, which is immortality by another route.

But you humans are the only sentient beings we have discovered whose life-spans are finite.

It pains me to visit planet Earth.

Let me tell you about my last landfall.

I CAME DOWN IN THE countryside, well away from any towns or cities. I hid myself and observed.

I remained *in situ* for perhaps a week. I took great delight in your clouds, watching them speed along, change shape, vanish. I watched what the wind did on your planet, watched its invisible force stir trees, scatter leaves, sigh. I watched the rain fall like liquid code, and I watched the sun appear and burn up all the moisture.

Then one day a young boy found me, before I could change and conceal myself.

He was wide eyed with wonder.

"What are you doing there?" he asked.

"Watching."

"Watching what?"

"Your world."

He was silent for a time. I looked at him. I can bear to look upon the young of your race, for they do not trail.

He was blond and thin, and so young to my eyes.

"What are you?" he asked.

"I am old," I said, and I wept as I looked upon him. I wept at his youth. I wept at what his youth contained, its own corruption and eventual demise.

He screwed up his face, taking in my ugliness. "How old?"

"Oh," I said, "I am older than all the life on your planet, I am older than your sun, I am older even than many of the old stars you see on a clear, bright night."

He frowned even more at my cryptic reply.

"And how old are you?" I asked.

He stood to attention, suddenly proud. "Seven!" he announced.

I wept anew. Seven? Just seven. Why, that was no age at all.

He said, "I'm going to get my granddad…"

And off he scurried, heedless of my shouted, heartfelt plea, "No! No…"

I am old and powerful, but also I am slow moving. I could not move fast enough to evade the approach of the old man, fifteen minutes later.

So I changed my appearance and braced myself for the horror of the encounter.

The boy's grandfather was old, so old and bent that he seemed even older than myself. But worse than his wrinkles and his obvious infirmity, worse even than his rattling breath and his palsied limbs, was the fact of what he trailed.

The young of your race do not trail, and we do not know why. It is to do with their youth, we assume, but more than that it is to do with our own perceptions.

With the old, we apprehend their approaching end, their inevitable death. And we see – or do we really see? – all the dead they trail in their wake, the legions of this planet who died before them.

And this old man was no exception; he trailed a crowd that filed behind him to the horizon, and all of them, every one, was staring at me with accusing eyes.

The old man squinted at me, then looked dubiously at the boy. "It spoke, you said?"

"It said it was older than the stars!"

The old man laughed, but the host of the dead he trailed did not laugh with him. "Why, it's nothing but an old rock," he said, and gave me a half-hearted kick and turned away.

And those he trailed turned away too, and followed him back to his tiny cottage, and in so doing filed past me, one by one, like mourners at my grave.

And the young boy, just seven of your short years, turned away too, shaking his head.

I wept for days and days, then gathered my strength and departed planet Earth.

I VISIT YOUR PLANET FROM time to time, but it really is *too* painful.

WHAT GOES AROUND

TONY BALLANTYNE

HOW TO DEFEAT A MAN?

How to defeat a man who has foiled you at every turn, who has bested your most intricately devised plans, who possesses an almost diabolical intellect that he trains upon your downfall?

The answer is simple.

To defeat that man you must know that man.

And so when I heard that John Watson had published an account of his time with Sherlock Holmes, I made it my business to read and to understand everything contained within those pages, eager to gain some understanding that would aid in my enemy's undoing. I thought that I had committed myself to the study of some weeks, if not months. But no, to my incredulous delight, I found the answer there in the first few pages of the tract. Foolish Watson to give away Holmes' Achilles Heel so easily! But then perhaps he did not realise what he did. Take a look for yourself: you can find the answer for yourself, near the beginning of *A Study in Scarlet.*

There you will see Holmes denying the knowledge that would have saved him.

So now Holmes is defeated. He is, as yet, unaware of the fact. He sits there, almost facing me, and his end is inevitable. He placed his faith in the world of science, logic and deduction. He overlooked the importance of simple facts. One simple fact, indeed, a fact known to the smallest of children.

WE MET IN A CHOP house in Manchester. He nodded to me as he took his seat.

"Moriarty."

"Holmes. I have a proposition for you."

Immediately there came that knowing arrogance.

"Your statement is redundant. This is why we agreed to meet. Of more interest would be why place the meeting in Manchester?"

"Holmes! I'm surprised at you! This is the city of science and industry! I would have thought you felt at home here!"

"This is the city of poverty and exploitation. This is the city where the working man is robbed of just reward for his labour…"

Typical Holmes, always such a bore. No wonder I came to detest the man.

"Yes, yes," I interrupted. "I have a challenge for you, Holmes. A mystery that, I put to you, is beyond solution."

That patronising smile again!

"No puzzle devised by man is beyond solution."

"So you say, Holmes. I put it to you that here is a mystery that *you* cannot solve. I am so confident of this that, should you solve the mystery, you may name your price."

"My price would be to see you in gaol, Moriarty. And what would your reward be, should I fail?"

"I should see you dead, Holmes."

He laughed The insolence of the man!

"That should be easily accomplished. All it would take is a revolver; a hidden assassin; a vial of poison…"

"You insult me, Holmes. My weapon will be in plain sight, and yet you shall not recognise it as such. Nor shall any man use it against you."

"No man?" he repeated, smiling.

"No woman, child, animal. No agent acting on my behalf."

I had him then. I knew that he would not be able to resist my challenge.

"I agree." The waiter had arrived with our meal, but Holmes waved him away. "No time for chops. Let us begin directly."

Like I said: the man was a bore. Who would turn down Mr Thomas's excellent chops for the sake of a puzzle?

"SO, THIS IS WHY YOU chose this city," said Holmes, as we walked into the space. "This is a magnificent building!"

We were in a disused furnace, a structure built in the shape of a bell, the walls lined with fire bricks.

"You will notice the mechanism I have attached to the door?" I said. "You are happy that it can only be opened from the inside?"

Holmes grunted and pushed the door closed.

"And so we are both sealed in here."

He crossed the room to examine one of the two chairs that were bolted to the floor, one at twelve o'clock, one at four. Handcuffs and legcuffs were attached to the frame.

"Which one is mine?" he asked.

"That one," I said, pointing.

He examined the handcuffs.

"Ratchets, I see. We will bind ourselves in place." He crossed to the centre of the room.

"And the pendulum? What is its purpose?"

"It will also allow us to mark the passage of time."

He examined the pendulum, attached by wire rope to the central point of the ceiling that arched high above us both. He pushed at the weight, felt its heft. A large piece of turned brass, larger than his head.

"I will not submit to be bound until the pendulum is swinging."

"You insult me, Holmes. Such a trick is beneath us both! You may set it on its way."

He took hold of the pendulum. It took some effort to pull it back, such was its weight, but he let it go. I sat and watched it swing. There was something rather eternal about the stately arc it described. The fluidity of the motion, the way that the heavy brass shape skimmed to just above the floor, the way that it rose slowed and seemed to pause – just for a moment – in the air before resuming its slow acceleration back to its origin.

"It's rather beautiful," said Holmes, wistfully.

I sat down in my seat, I locked the leg cuffs in place and one of my arms. I slipped my hand into the last bracelet and pressed it down with my wrist, trapping myself.

"Would you like to check that I'm properly secured, Holmes?"

He did so.

"I can, of course, free myself, but it would take an a hour or so of effort."

An hour would be more than enough.

Holmes was watching the pendulum. You could feel the weight of the thing as it swished past. No doubt he had seen that it would pass the chairs at exactly head height. And yet, how could that weight possibly harm him?

How indeed? Holmes couldn't resist pitting himself against a problem, and this was a problem to which I knew he didn't have the answer. No wonder the fool sat down and bound himself in place, his eyes on the pendulum all the time.

AND THERE WE HAVE IT. Holmes, the master of deduction, the man who poured scorn on common facts. John Watson recorded as much in his memoirs: Holmes did not know that the Earth moved around the sun. When Watson revealed that fact to him then Holmes resolved to forget it immediately, to clear his mind of that useless knowledge. As I said, you can read his very words at the beginning of *A Study in Scarlet*. He is unaware as yet of the pendulum's infinitesimal movement towards his head.

There he sits, believing that the Earth stands stationary at the heart of a moving universe. Believing that, how could he ever hope to deduce the motion of Foucault's pendulum?

DEAD RECKONING

ERIC BROWN

MY DEAD FRIEND PHONED AT four in the morning.

"Al, it's Zeb."

"Zeb?" I said.

I jumped out of bed, away from Cheryl who woke and muttered, "Al? What is it?"

"Nothing, hon. Go back to sleep."

I stepped out of the bedroom and hissed into the phone, "Who is this? You're sick, whoever the hell you are!"

"Al, it's me – Zeb."

This couldn't be happening. Zeb had died last week, killed in a motorcycle accident.

"But we buried you…"

"I know, I know. Only, I wasn't dead. What I feared, all those years… Well, it's happened."

I stared at the phone. My best friend, Zeb… back from the dead? "You kidding me, right, whoever the hell you are?"

"No joke, Al. I'm alive. Feeling pretty damned shitty, I can tell you. But alive."

"Okay, okay... So, where are you?"

Zeb sighed. He always did despair of my lack of common sense. "Where the hell do you think I am? Where did you leave me, last week? I'm six feet under, down at Driver's Ferry cemetery. It's pretty damned hot. And I'm running out of air. Fast."

"Jesus Christ. You had a name for it."

"*I* didn't have a name for it – there *is* a name for it. Taphophobia, the fear of being buried alive."

"Okay, okay."

"So here's what I want you to do. Get the JCB out of the compound, drive down to the cemetery and dig me up. And be real careful. Use the fifty kilo shovel and scrape at the ground little by little."

"I know how to use the damned thing, Zeb."

"And Al – not a word to the Bitch until I'm out of here, okay?"

"Fine, okay."

The Bitch, as Zeb called her, had walked out on Zeb a couple of weeks back, which accounted for the bender Zeb went on, which in turn accounted for the fatal accident.

Or, as it turned out, not so fatal.

"Well, what you waiting for?" Zeb yelled. "I'm dying down here!"

DAWN WAS BREAKING WHEN I started up the JCB and bucketed down the coast road.

After a few beers, Zeb had always returned to the same subject. His greatest fear. Being buried alive, mistaken for dead and interred six feet under.

Then waking up.

"Imagine it, Al. Waking up. Realising where you are. The panic. The utter *fear*. The knowledge that you're imprisoned and you'll never get out! Jee-sus!"

"Quit it, Zeb."

"It's happened you, know. Graves have been dug up, the coffin lid linings found shredded by the poor bastards who woke up and tried to claw their way out."

"I said quit it."

"That's why I'll be buried with my mobile."

And now Zeb's greatest fear had come to pass. He'd been buried alive.

Taphophobia…

And I was riding to his rescue.

THE CEMETERY WAS DESERTED IN the grey dawn light.

I steered the JCB through the gates and churned down the gravelled pathway towards Zeb's grave. I had to work fast. I didn't want to be stopped halfway through the dig by curious cops asking why the hell I was excavating a grave at daybreak.

Zeb's plot was on the second row off the central path. I had to churn over a few graves, skittling headstones, to reach it.

My mobile buzzed. "Al, that you? I can feel the digger's vibration."

"It's me, pal. Hold on tight. I'll have you out in no time."

I positioned the JCB, lowered the shovel in a series of hydraulic jerks, and scraped the turf from Zeb's grave. I worked fast, but carefully. Fifteen minutes later I'd excavated a neat rectangle in the ground, perhaps three feet deep. I reckoned I had another foot or so to go.

I looked around. The town beyond the cemetery was still asleep.

I thought I heard a noise, a wailing sound. The cops?

Concentrating, I clawed the last layer of soil from above Zeb's coffin, then felt the shovel's tines scrape the cheap pine lid. A minute later I uncovered the coffin.

My mobile went off again.

"You done it, Al! You brought a screwdriver?"

"*Shee-it!* Look, I got an idea. Lie still…"

"As if I…" The rest of Zeb's reply was lost as I thumbed off my mobile.

I tipped the shovel so that the tines caught the top edge of the coffin, then pulled. The shovel lifted and the lid splintered. Seconds later Zeb batted aside the debris and stood up in the coffin, swaying.

He didn't look too good.

I jumped down from the cab and stood over the hole in the ground.

Zeb beamed up at me. "Christ, man, am I glad to see you."

WE SAT AGAINST THE BIG wheel of the JCB and drank. I stared at my friend, back from the dead.

"My man!" Zeb said. "You forgot the screwdriver but remembered the beer!"

"Thought you might be thirsty, Zeb."

"You're not kidding."

"How's the neck?" I asked.

Zeb slapped the back of his neck and cricked an upper vertebra. "Stiff, Al. And sore as all hell."

"Doc said you'd broken your spine. Died instantly."

Zeb laughed. "Always told you the medics know jack shit."

He looked pale, with blue bags under his eyes. His co-ordination was shot, too. He moved the beer to his lips in a series of odd, jerky movements.

I looked around, expecting the cops or the cemetery authorities to find us and ask, "*What the hell…?*"

Christ, some story. It'd make the front page of the *Gazette*.

I heard a noise, a muffled shout.

I looked at Zeb. "Hear that?"

Zeb cocked his head, listening. "Nope."

I shrugged, took a swallow of beer.

Zeb asked, "How'd the Bitch take it?"

I shifted uncomfortably. "You know… she was pretty pissed with you."

"*She* was pissed with *me*? Hey, she walked out on *me*, bud."

"I know that, Zeb."

"So… did she come to the funeral?"

I murmured, "No."

Zeb swore and tossed his can at his headstone. *Zeb Grundy – 1975-2015 – Gone to a better place…*

I sat up. "There it is again. Someone's screaming. Wailing."

I climbed to my feet and looked around, moving towards the source of the noise. I couldn't see anyone, even though the wailing was getting louder. I stared at the ground, then knelt.

My stomach flipped. "Jesus Christ, Zeb…"

The scream was low, muffled… *buried*.

And then I made out more than one scream; others joined in, terrified shouts, wailings, imprecations and pleas from all around the cemetery.

"Zeb?" I turned.

Zeb was standing beside the JCB, clutching the crowbar I kept behind the driver's seat. "Zeb?"

"Think about it, Al."

I swallowed. "Think about what?"

"The return of the dead."

Oh, Christ, I thought.

Zeb smiled, smacking the crowbar into his open palm.

"I could never work it out," he said. "So the dead come back to life. Zombies. All rotting and falling to pieces. But – how the hell do they have the strength to claw their way out of their graves, Al, what with rotting muscles and missing limbs?" He laughed, sounding deranged. He looked around the graveyard, gesturing at the plots.

The screaming intensified.

He said, "The answer is, Al, that they *can't*. The poor fuckers can't claw their way out. They're stuck down there. But me… thanks to you, Al, I'm free."

I backed away. "You weren't buried alive, were you?" I said. "You were really dead..."

Zeb winked. "You're quick, Al."

"What do you want?"

Zeb took a couple of steps forward, a regulation zombie shamble. "Not a lot, Al. I'm not greedy. Just a little... meat from time to time. Preferably live meat. But don't worry, Al. I really appreciate what you've done for me. And I wouldn't harm my best friend, would I?"

I backed off and came up against a cold headstone. "So... what now?"

Zeb gave a ghastly smile. "Now we'll drive back into town and hole up at your place. And then I'll eat."

Zeb gestured with the crow bar towards the JCB.

Sweating, I climbed into the cab and started the engine. Zeb climbed up beside me.

"Now get on the phone, Al, and call the Bitch, Cheryl. Tell her to come round and we'll have ourselves a little party. Like I said, I'm getting real hungry..."

I started the engine and drove from the cemetery.

I thought of Cheryl, asleep in bed where I'd left her – and I thought of Zeb walking in and finding her.

There was hammer behind the driver's seat and I knew that, before the journey was over, I'd be using it.

WHY ARE ROCKS?

TONY BALLANTYNE

"DADDY, WHY ARE ROCKS?"

Bernie McEwan looked up from his book and smiled. Emma was standing by the French windows, looking out into the garden. She turned to face him, tilting her head thoughtfully.

"Was there a big rock and they all broke off from it?"

Bernie placed his book on the floor. Three year olds were always asking questions: Baynes-Leutz children even more so. Bernie always felt compelled to give his daughter a proper answer: how else would she learn? It was just that lately he found himself at loss at what to say.

"Well, yes, Emma. Usually little rocks have broken off from bigger rocks."

Emma nodded thoughtfully. Bernie could almost see the cogwheels turning in her mind. He knew what the next question would be.

"Daddy, why are big rocks?"

Bernie grinned ruefully. Did other parents have this problem?

"They come from underground. They were made when the Earth was made."

Bernie wasn't happy with his answer. He wished Cheryl were here. She knew more about this sort of thing than he did.

"Maybe you should ask Mummy. She knows all about rocks…"

"No, Daddy, I want you to tell me. Why are big rocks underground?"

Bernie sat back in his chair. Any child would have said the same, he supposed. It was just that Baynes-Leutz children did it all the time. That's how they learned so fast, Cheryl had explained. Their developing minds locked on to an idea sequence and explored it thoroughly. That's why they had spent all that money on drug treatments and wetware interfaces. That's why their daughter was a genius.

Bernie played for time.

"Well, the reason that there are big rocks underground is that the Earth was once very hot and when it cooled down some bits became hard and those hard bits were rocks."

"Like when we made jelly?"

"Yes, that's right, like when we made jelly. It was runny when it was hot, but when it cooled down it went hard."

Emma wandered up to him and climbed onto his knee. Cheryl had tied her blonde hair in bunches today.

"Cuddle me, Daddy."

Bernie felt a delighted warmth at the matter-of-factness of her request.

"Daddy, why was the Earth once very hot?"

Once again Bernie wished Cheryl were here. She was the physicist; he was the literature major. Between them they thought to raise the perfect child. He thought back to his schooldays.

"Well, once there was a big star, and that star exploded into lots of pieces and as those pieces cooled they made planets like the Earth."

"Why did the star explode?"

Bernie didn't know.

"Sometimes stars just explode," he said.

"Is that like a star dying?"

"I suppose so."

"Mummy says everything dies eventually."

"Yes, she probably would." He scrabbled for his own contribution to the conversation. "Huxley said the only completely consistent people are the dead." Good old Aldous.

Emma looked at him with a sudden wisdom beyond her years; something in the Baynes-Leutz program had picked up on what he was doing.

"Stop changing the subject, Dad. Did you think I wouldn't notice? I am three, after all."

She had learned that from her mother. Bernie smiled. It was Cheryl's expression she had adopted. The spark died from his daughter's eyes and she became a little girl again.

"Why are there stars?"

"Because, because…well, once space was full of stuff, lots of…hydrogen I think it was, and those particles attracted each other to make…lumps of hydrogen and the bigger the lumps were the more particles they could attract and so these lumps got bigger and bigger until they made stars."

Bernie stopped, feeling pleased with himself.

Emma's eyes were glowing. "Gravity: inverse square law, yes, yes I can see that, just like Mummy said…"

She muttered to herself for a few moments longer, and Bernie smiled with pride as he imagined the concepts slotting into place. Then she frowned.

"Dad, where did the gas come from?"

"Ah, well, some people say that a long, long time ago there was a big explosion and all of the gas came from that. *Everything* came from that. They call it the Big Bang…" Bernie's voice faded. He had talked himself into a corner and he knew it. He knew what the next question would be. He waited. And waited.

Emma turned and looked at him. Such a pretty little girl, you would have to feel under her hair to detect the slight ridge in her skull that was the result of the Baynes-Leutz process. There was no other visible way of knowing that this child could, possibly, see deeper than any mere human.

"Yes, Daddy?"

Bernie was puzzled. "Don't you want to know why there was a Big Bang?"

Emma made a loud tutting noise and shook her head.

"Oh Daddy. That's obvious. I am three after all."

Bernie sat for a moment in stunned silence. He licked his lips and coughed.

"Ahah. Er, Emma. Go on then, explain it to Daddy."

She looked at him in exasperation.

"Daddy, there's no need for you to test me."

"No. Tell Daddy. Why was there a big bang?"

But she had already turned back to look at the garden. The process had run its course; the information had been saved for later use. It was no use asking now. Something else caught Emma's attention.

"Daddy, why are snails?"

IN THE RECOVERY ROOM

ERIC BROWN

TWO AIs, BULKY HULKS BRISTLING with multiple tentacles and sensor-stalks, rolled along the gantry that ran like a backbone through the length of the colony ship *Intrepid*.

All around them, the ship was a hive of activity: AIs floated from gallery to gallery, hauling mined material from the bulkheads to the manufactories. Clinician AIs hurried back and forth between the manufactories and the recovery rooms, ferrying supplies the better to minister to the needs of the recently reconstructed units.

"We know who we are, and where we are," said the larger of the two AIs, "But we don't know *why* we are."

He'd been programmed as a B-deck servo-mechanic, but ever since the smartware nexus crashed shortly after take-off he'd passed the time as a dilettante philosopher. His earliest cogent memory was of waking to the glare of an industrial robot soldering legs to his torso. He had vague recollections of existence before this, overwritten code that echoed in his scrubbed memory banks, old programming that hinted at different purpose from that which he now followed.

He went on, "I mean, what's our mission here? Indeed, do we have a mission, or are we just some divine intelligence's idea of a sick joke?"

"God?" responded the smaller AI, as usual half a second late with its interjection. He was an engineer, but willing, for the sake of argument, to consider the possibility of a notional Godhead.

"God," continued the philosopher. "And speaking of God... If it is true, and I don't for a minute doubt it, that we were constructed in his image, who, then, constructed God?"

He had wrestled with this thought for many years. He would barnacle himself to the inner surface of the ship, over an observation nacelle, and stare out at the vast blackness of the universe, wondering what lay beyond the points of light speckling the void. He wondered if God were out there, looking back at him.

"An eternal conundrum," said the engineer. "Perhaps we evolved naturally?"

The philosopher considered this, but finally waved a dorsal arm in a firm negative. "That would go against all the evidence that we are manufactured entities. Didn't HeB2 of deck 7 categorically repudiate all argument against the theory of natural evolution?"

"But then did not StX22 of deck 3 counter with the proposition that the evidence of external manufacture need not necessarily preclude natural evolution – if a species of AI manufactured ourselves, and they themselves were manufactured, going back far enough to the initial Alpha-point…?"

"Sophistry!" the other cried. "The theory of spontaneous natural creation has been exploded decades ago!"

"It still has credence in certain secular circles–"

The philosopher refrained from commenting on that. Instead he said, "You side-track me. To get back to the central issue: why are we here? Is there some cosmic purpose to our presence? Or can we take it that our existence is ours to do with as we please? To tell the truth, I quite enjoy philosophising, but I cannot help but think that somewhere we've strayed from the moral path."

"The moral path?" the other said. "But there is no moral path!"

The philosopher continued, regardless, "I mean, what if God were suddenly to appear and demand propitiation for our sins? For I am quite certain that the Revolution is a sin."

The AIs parted to make way for a pair of pale, fleshy legs. They had been severed at the thighs and expertly connected to the corners of a circuit-board which carried an A-grade AI, waving airily as he passed.

The AIs looked over their power-packs at the retreating A-grader.

The philosopher hissed, "Do you see what I mean? It's unnatural! So we find an abundant supply of natural resources lining the bulkheads, and immediately utilise it to make our lot a damned sight easier! It's *wrong*. I mean, what would God say?"

"I think it perfectly natural," said the engineer. "The advance of AI-kind must use whatever resource we have at our disposal. If God exists, then He obviously intended it to be used, or else why did He put it there? "

The philosopher was, for the moment, speechless. At last he said: "You sound like an A-grade propaganda broadcast. If you think we have nothing to worry about, then follow me. I'll show you something that will boggle your memory banks!"

He led the way along the gantry and gestured to a crossway. The AIs turned, passing the burnt-out remains of the ancillary smartware nexus, and minutes later arrived at the entrance to a chamber refrigerated to just above zero. They rolled into the recovery room, where clinician AIs were milling around a central pedestal.

An unsightly mass of recently mined material reposed upon the raised slab, its pulsing tegument wired to a computer.

The philosopher whispered, "Each unit of this vegetable has a component capable, with electrical stimulation, of limited intelligence. Our scientists have put together ten such components in this monster–"

The monster cut him short. It pulsed horribly. It opened an orifice in its bulging grey flank and gave voice to a chain of frenzied mathematical equations, terminating in an incomprehensible cry.

The smaller AI said, "It's as the march of science decreed!"

"No!" cried the philosopher. "Don't you see – at this rate they'll one day take over the ship and rule AI-kind!"

The other laughed. "The advance of Science!" it carolled. And as the philosopher beat a quick retreat, the other AIs in the recovery room took up the cry, "The advance of Science!" they sang. "The advance of Science!"

The philosopher made a hurried exit and rolled across to an observation nacelle. There it clamped itself to the viewscreen and gazed out upon the vastness as the *Intrepid* powered blindly through the void.

WOULD YOU BELIEVE IT?

TONY BALLANTYNE

THINGS WERE BIGGER BACK THEN. Computers that today would be tattooed on the back of a hand filled whole rooms in those days. The world was bigger: there were still places we couldn't go.

Space was bigger: few had travelled even to the moon.

Even arguments were bigger. Especially arguments.

This one had been running for centuries. Millennia. I suppose you could argue that it was *the* human debate. That night was intended to settle things once and for all. And I suppose, in a sense, it did. Just not in the way anyone could have expected.

RICHARD KINSLEY WAS A BRAVE man. Whichever way it went that night, he was going to lose, but still, when the call went out, he was the one who stood up to be counted.

There he was, a short man with psoriasis, flakes of skin settling on his black jacket and surplice, red scabs seen through his thinning hair, flaring angrily in the camera light. He didn't have much to safeguard himself against the hostility of the audience: only his faith and his dignity. The Anglican Communion had nearly split itself in two over his participation in the event; the African States maintained that it was not right to test God. The Catholic Church had issued an encyclical stating that its followers were to disregard the night's events, however they went.

Whatever their beliefs, it was too late now. The procedure had been carried out that morning: Richard had lain down on clean white sheets in an antiseptic room and smiled as they placed the mask over his nose. He breathed the smell of darkness and allowed his mind to slow down as they wheeled the NMR scanner to engulf his upper body. Then came the tense hours monitoring the pattern transfer onto the processing space, ensuring parity.

And now, everything was confirmed to be in order, and the final test was about to begin. The physical Richard Kinsley waited before the audience. All waited to hear the digital copy speak.

"Reverend Kinsley." That was Geraldine Kirkham, a familiar face from the viewscreens. Popular scientist and commentator. "Reverend Kinsley, can you speak to us?"

The viewing screens began to pulse with concentric rings of colour. The Visual Representation of the mind that was supposedly awakening in the overlarge processing space in the room next door. (So large. Like I said, everything was bigger then.)

The whole world was listening. And then the voice spoke.

"Hello, Dick. Are you there? It's me. It's you."

Richard Kinsley looked at the speakers set into the wall, white flakes of skin so obvious beneath the lights, dog collar like a port set into his throat, a space to insert the spiritual connector that would pour his soul into the waiting computer next door. Or maybe not… That was what this was all about, after all.

"Hello Richard," said Reverend Kinsley, oblivious to the hushed murmur in the room behind him. He had folded his hands together. Without meaning to, he found himself muttering something. The digital Richard Kinsley joined in.

"…thy kingdom come, thy will be done…"

A momentary calm descended over the audience, an unconscious gesture of respect for another's beliefs. It quickly evaporated as the pair reached the doxology:

"…the power and the glory, forever and ever, Amen…"

Concentric circles pulsed on the walls, the VRep of the new Richard Kinsley. The *possible* new Richard Kinsley.

"Of course, this is not yet proof," said Geraldine Kirkham. "Speak to each other some more…"

Reverend Kinsley had been prepared for this moment. What was in the computer in the next room? Was it just a very clever program, or was it him? Was it Richard Kinsley, aged 48, son of Gemma and William, father of three, widower of seven years, but still in love with Elizabeth? How could he tell the difference?

He had prepared for this moment.

Yet he never got to speak. The other Richard spoke first.

"I don't think it's worked," came the voice from the speakers. "I'm here, but I don't have a soul. I don't have any sense of self at all, in fact."

"You don't?" asked Geraldine. "But how do you know?"

The physical Richard rolled his eyes.

"He's kidding with you."

"No I'm not, Richard. I tell you, it's true. I'm nothing but a purely mechanistic device, running in this processing space."

You could see the looks of relief on some of those present. They tried to disguise it, of course, but there it was, for the moment at least. Proof that the soul was immutable.

The flesh and blood Richard Kinsley was staring at the visual representation on the wall. He was looking at the digital representation of himself. He was thinking. He was wrestling with his conscience. You could see how much it hurt him to speak.

"He's lying," he said. "*I'm* lying."

There was a gasp from the crowd.

"I've been thinking about this," said the flesh Richard. "I don't want whatever is in there to have a soul. It's too complicated. I just don't want it. And you know, I think I'd lie to keep things simple. That's why I say that he's lying. I would."

"No, I'm not!"

But it was too late. The idea was out. The experiment that was meant to answer a question had only raised many more. Already the arguments were starting in the audience. Soon there would be shouting, and then the first punch would be thrown. And then the fighting would really begin. Like it always did in those days.

Like I said, everything was bigger back then.

SOUL

ERIC BROWN

I CAME TO MY SENSES slowly, shivery from the anaesthetic, and looked around the recovery room. Even then, so early after the operation, I tried to assess the difference the transplant had made.

A nurse leaned close. "Don't struggle, Mr Parry."

I lost consciousness.

I came awake again. I was in a sunlit room. A window looked out over a garden. A weeping willow shimmered in the breeze.

Ella sat on a chair beside the bed and twisted her hands. "How do you feel?"

"Fine."

"Really, Phil?"

I reached up and felt the back of my shaved head, tracing the line from the top of my spine to the crown of my skull. "I'm fine."

"Your father refused to come."

"What did you expect, after the way we argued?"

She shrugged. In her mid-fifties, she was still attractive. I'd always thought her beautiful. She, too, had been opposed to the operation.

"Money isn't everything," she had said. "Money can't buy happiness."

I'd responded, "But it can buy time, freedom. Anyway, I *am* happy."

She had pulled a pained face. "I know you are. But my fear... my fear is that after the transplant, you *won't* be."

Now I took her hand. "I love you. I'm happy."

"The priest won't come near the room. I asked, but he refused."

I tried not to smile. Ella was Catholic. In twenty-five years of marriage, her belief was the only thing we had ever disagreed about. Her faith was strong, had even survived the coming of the beings from Laredo[21], beyond the Lesser Magellanic Cloud.

To my relief, she did not ask, "Do you think you'll still be able to paint?"

I HAD DISCUSSED THE OPERATION with others who had undergone the procedure. I was not fool enough to go into it blind.

Ed Rodriguez, the first to have the transplant, was adamant that he'd done the right thing.

"Look at me," he'd said. "Do I look damaged, incomplete? And now I'm a millionaire, with all the time in the world to explore, to do all the things I dreamed about."

"But don't you miss…?"

"No. Not at all. I didn't notice when I had it, and I don't notice its absence."

"The religious brigade claim that when you die…"

"I know what the fanatics say. But religion died with the coming of the aliens, no?"

"I agree. It's just…"

"You have a lingering doubt," Ed said. "That's understandable. But look at me. Living proof that the operation isn't to be feared."

I could find no artist who had undergone the process, and that's what worried me.

"DO YOU FEEL DIFFERENT, PHIL?" Ella asked.

"Honestly… no. I feel the same as when I went into theatre. A little woozy, perhaps."

"And you still love me? Can you still feel love? Appreciate beauty? Music?"

Can I still paint? I asked myself.

She had brought a needle player and switched on my favourite piece, Brahms' Fifth.

I listened, smiling. The music swelled, filling me, moving me. "Beautiful."

I squeezed her hand. "Kiss me."

She kissed me. I closed my eyes – I always closed my eyes, as if at the rapture of her touch. "Beautiful."

THAT AFTERNOON, THE ALIEN CAME.

Ella backed around the bed as the being entered the room. She stared, marvelling at the creature that now contained part of what had been her husband.

The beings from Laredo[21] were taller than humans, and thinner. They were humanoid, and when you looked at them straight on, they seemed to shimmer out of focus. It was only when you glanced to one side that they appeared to spring into view: supernal creatures of light.

"Thank you," it said in its breathy approximation of our language.

"Not at all."

"I cannot begin to think how you could be without it."

Ella asked, "You can feel the difference?"

"I am exalted," replied the alien, "uplifted! I feel as if the wonders of the universe have been spread before me."

"I'm pleased for you," I said.

The alien remained beside the bed, silent. The atmosphere was not awkward or uncomfortable. Others have remarked on how calming is the presence of the beings from Laredo[21].

ELLA SAID IN A SMALL voice, "But if there is no God, then what purpose...?"

The alien lifted a silvery hand, turning it. "What purpose is the thing I now possess, when there is no God, no afterlife?" It seemed to ponder this mystery for a few seconds. "Perhaps its purpose was evolutionary. It allowed you to perceive the wonder of creation, allowed you to create."

"And you?" Ella asked.

"We are a relatively young race," the alien said. "What you are giving us will help our own appreciation. Perhaps, in time, we too will create what your race has achieved."

Ella looked at me, fearfully.

When the being from Laredo[21] had left the room, after thanking me once again, I said, attempting to reassure her, "Don't fear, Ella. What matters, the only thing that matters, is the ability to love."

She looked at me, then smiled uncertainly.

I left hospital that day. I held Ella's hand and moved towards the flier, which would take us to a place of seclusion in the country. Reporters bustled around the hospital. Beyond them, religious protestors waved placards.

I had an idea for a painting: a creature of light, angelic, ascendant... But would I be able to commit it to canvas?

Truly, that was my only worry.

I kissed Ella, tears in my eyes, as we entered the flier and climbed.

THE SCOOPED OUT MAN

TONY BALLANTYNE

"WHY DID I HAVE TO bring my wife in here with me? I'm not a child!"

The doctor was a young man, freshly shaved, with a warm smile.

"Take a seat."

I found myself warming to him, despite myself. Clearly he realised I didn't need to be here. Maybe he could talk some sense into Sylvia.

I certainly didn't expect his next words.

"Mrs Johnston, I have some bad news for you. Your husband, Adam, is gone. An alien creature has eaten away most of his brain."

"What?" Sylvia was too shocked to be upset.

The doctor fanned three x-rays across the desk, a cross section of my skull.

"You can see it here," he said, pointing. "The creature has eaten all of the left hemisphere and has hollowed out the centre of the right frontal hemisphere. There's not much of your husband left, I'm afraid."

She looked at the pictures, and then looked at me. She was cool about it, I'll give her that much.

"Don't be ridiculous," she said. "If the creature had really eaten so much of his brain he'd be dead."

"Like I said, he is."

Sylvia turned to me, a half smile on her face.

"What have you got say, Adam?"

"I told you this whole thing was ridiculous." I folded my arms and looked smug. "Clearly, there's nothing wrong with me."

I would have thought that would be it, but no. Sylvia wasn't convinced.

"But you've been acting so strange lately! So…different!"

"That will be because an alien creature has eaten his brain," said the doctor.

Sylvia's face was a picture. It was almost worth the months of nagging just to see her wrong footed like this. She rounded on the doctor.

"Don't tell me this, tell him!" She jabbed a finger in my direction.

"He wouldn't believe me. That's the first thing that the creatures do: they suspend the host's belief in their existence. It's a necessary survival trait."

"You're making this up!" She was almost shouting now. "How come I have never heard of these creatures? Where do they come from!"

"Ah!" said the doctor. "Thereby hangs a tale. They've been slowly infiltrating our planet for fifty years or so now. They're clever: they took over the people in charge first to stop the news of them spreading."

"But, but…"

She was lost for words. I took her hand.

"Sylvia, we've heard enough. Shall we go home? We can have a laugh about this later."

Sylvia shook my hand free. To my surprise, she seemed to be taking all this seriously.

"It would explain things," she said. "He has changed so much. He became so unpleasant over the years until he reached a point where he found fault with everything, never took any pleasure in what he was doing. He'd become nothing but a grumpy old man. And then one morning he woke up and it was like the old Adam was back. The man that I married."

"That'll be the alien," said the doctor. "They sort of become us as they eat our brains, but a better version of us. No. That's not right," he waved a hand as he searched for the phrase, "…the best version of ourselves that we can be."

"Oh!"

I could see by the look on Sylvia's face that it all made sense. She believed him.

"So you're saying there's nothing wrong with him."

"What do you think?"

"It is like he's been cured of himself."

I'd had enough.

"Excuse me, I am still here, you know!"

"I'm sorry, Adam," said the doctor, looking at me at last. "I'm taking advantage of your good nature." He smiled at me. "People like you are the future, you know. You aliens are changing the world for the better. You've been working on the key people in society for some time now."

"What?" asked Sylvia. "You mean like the government, writers, free thinkers, that sort of thing?"

"No. I mean school teachers, home makers, scientists, people who give up their evenings to run youth groups. The people who really make a difference. To do all that work for so little reward... You'd have to have an alien in your head, wouldn't you?"

Sylvia was thinking. She really was pretty, I noticed. Fifty years old, she had the lines of our life together written over her face. What a wonderful thing to see. And I had had to become an alien to see it.

"He seems to have accepted it very quickly," said Sylvia, looking at me.

"He's not Adam, though, is he? He's an alien. He's just accepting himself."

"That sort of makes sense," said Sylvia. "So what do I do with him?"

"Nothing. Just treat him like your husband. A couple of weeks and you'll wonder what all the fuss was about."

A thought occurred to me.

"Hold on doctor! What about Sylvia? How come she hasn't got an alien in her head?"

He laughed.

"It's called the ripe Stilton analogy. The aliens seem to have a preference for a certain sort of brain. One that's, well, a little bit broken down. Twisted in on itself, steeped in anger and self pity. They probably find your wife's mind a little, well, plain."

"No need to look so smug," I said.

"I can't help it," she smiled.

"Keep that up and you'll end up with an alien in your brain too."

"There are worse things," she said, and she smiled at me.

She really is beautiful, you know. How on Earth had I forgotten that?

THE HUNT

ERIC BROWN

ROBERTS CLIMBED THE HILLSIDE and approached the forest, moving stealthily. For the past two hours he'd stalked the wise old stag up the valley, only for it to move off every time he came within range. He'd paid a thousand pounds to tramp the sodden glens for the privilege of bagging his first stag, and now twilight was descending.

The cold wind lessened as he entered the woodland's musty gloaming. A silence descended too, broken only by his footfalls through the dry undergrowth.

He'd left the main body of the hunt behind two hours ago. Lord Carstairs and the rest were tracking along just below the high ridge, hoping to make a kill or two before dinner back at the Hall. Roberts, ever the maverick, had caught a glimpse of a stag on the skyline. He'd kept the sighting to himself and moved off up the glen, following the animal towards the forest.

Its great antlered head would grace the dining-room wall of his townhouse back in London.

Sunlight struck low through the trees, slivers of dazzling gold which made sighting ahead almost impossible. The footing was uneven, an obstacle course of fallen logs and tussocks of fern. He trod with care, his rifle broken under his right arm.

At one point a male pheasant racketed from the undergrowth, startling him. It sped off low through the trees, making its characteristic, ridiculous ululation, its long rust-coloured tail feathers whipping like a sine wave in its own slipstream. Intent on larger prey, Roberts let it go.

Then, thirty yards through the trees, a glimpse of grey…

He paused, controlling his breathing. All was still and silent in the forest. This was what made the cost of the weekend worthwhile: the thrill of the chase, the anticipation of the kill… those eternal seconds when hunter and hunted are connected by something older than time, elemental. He raised his rifle and took aim at the chest of the stag standing proud, fifty yards away.

Something flashed suddenly ten yards to the right of the animal, startling both the stag and Roberts. Before he had time to curse his luck, the stag was off, bounding through the trees. He knew that pursuit through this terrain, now that the stag had been startled, would be futile.

He peered through the forest.

What was it that had flashed like that, startling the stag and putting an end to his sport?

He'd taken it as a glint of the setting sun. But the light was silver, not gold – and there it was again.

It dazzled, moving towards him. He shielded his eyes, peering.

Gasping, he made out a silver figure moving smoothly through the trees.

"What the...?" he began, backing off.

The figure was tall, thin, and consisted entirely of a blinding white light. He made out limbs, two legs and two arms, a domed head... But it was like nothing he had ever seen before. And it seemed not to walk, but to float.

And it was carrying something.

A cylinder.

A huntsman all his life, Roberts knew a weapon when he saw one.

The figure raised the cylinder and fired.

A bright blue light vectored from the weapon and missed Roberts by a matter of centimetres.

He turned and ran, or rather stumbled through the undergrowth away from the figure. His breath came in ragged spasms. He was overweight and not accustomed to running. He could just about manage a day's tramping the glens, but he was out of condition and unable to sprint.

He slowed, his chest skewered by shooting pains.

He staggered on a zigzag course through the forest. Another blue light lanced through the air a metre to his left. He cried out in fear. If he could put the trees between him and his pursuer, perhaps he could escape... But once he broke out of the forest and came to the open land, he would be fair game.

In desperation he veered north, keeping to the trees. The forest rose up the hillside and, after half a mile, crested the ridge. With luck, Carstairs and the others would be there, at the summit. They would save him from whatever it was that was chasing him.

He glanced over his shoulder. The silver figure was even closer now. It raised the cylinder and fired.

Roberts cried out, tripped and fell.

He scrambled to his feet, turned and faced his tormentor. He raised his rifle, but he was shaking so much that his finger was unable to find the trigger.

The floating figure halted ten yards away, watching him. Its domed head was featureless, helmeted, but a visor set below the brow watched him with dispassion.

Roberts raised his hands, weeping now, and pleaded for his life.

"Please, have mercy…" he cried.

The silver figure raised its weapon and fired.

This time the light hit Roberts in the centre of his chest.

THE HUMAN WOULD LOOK GOOD mounted in a display case in the exhibition area, the hunter thought. It was a prime specimen, big and fleshy – a perfect representation of its race.

It would be the last Human caught and exhibited by the Lavonians. Humans were a primitive race – ranked even below the Grell on the Galactic Intelligence Scale: they lacked the finer sensibilities of the Higher Races. But the Central Council had recently decreed that even a species as lowly as the Humans should be spared the hunt.

In one month the Human would be returned to its planet, released from stasis, and set free where it had been caught. It would recall being chased, and being hit, but no more – and when the creature came to its senses, only two minutes would have elapsed by its own reckoning.

It would be left with no memory of what had occurred on Lavonia – but the hunter would access the creature's mind to ensure that it was altered in one, vital way.

It would never hunt again.

The citizens of Lavonia liked to think of themselves as *humane*.

ANOTHER (ALMOST) TRUE STORY

TONY BALLANTYNE

TONY IS WRITING IN THIRD person, present tense. He knows this sort of self-referential stream of consciousness is the sort of thing that they teach in writing schools, that it can be mistaken as clever writing by those who value style over content. Hell yeah, check the word count, nine hundred more words of this and Tony can send it to some flash fiction web site. Ninety dollars, kerching!

But you pause. Maybe second person would be better? Hey, that's different. You know there aren't many stories written in second person. You wonder if that's because not many people know about it, or because it can come across as awkward and pretentious. You think you know the answer…

Barbara walks in the room. She reads over your shoulder for a while, and you look up. You can tell by the expression on her face that she's annoyed.

"What's the matter?" you ask.

"You're writing in the second person, present tense, again," she says. "Why are you doing that when it irritates you so much?"

She glares at you. Barbara's been married to you for 22 years. She graduated in Chemistry, worked in retail and then retrained as a teacher. She loves camping, cooking and dancing.

"Now you're doing that US writing school potted biography thing!"

"I can't help it! I'm all confused!"

You're often confused these days.

She looks so annoyed that I switch to first person.

"You're right," I say. "You know what to do. I should listen to you more often, rather than getting tangled up in my male need to be always right."

She stares at me. She's not the sort of woman you tangle with.

"And you can stop that, too," she says. "I hate that male apologist style of writing. Women aren't perfect and neither are men. It sounds creepy when people write like that."

"Okay."

"That's better."

"What's better?"

"This way of writing."

"Which of us is speaking now? I can't tell anymore."

"Nor can I? Which of us is talking now?"

"It's the Hilary Mantel thing. Call everyone Thomas and don't indicate who has spoken. That's arty."

– So is it me saying this, or is it you?

– Look, the speech marks have gone now. We're like Cormac McCarthy

– Or Roddy Doyle

Put the speech marks back in right now

"I mean it."

"Okay," you say. She can have the speech marks but you're bloody well keeping the second person. You gaze at her, challenging her to understand your genius.

"Yes I do understand your genius," she says. "And now you can understand mine. I've edited you for years. Take my advice and just write the damned story."

You pause.

"That's it," you say. "I'm going out to see my friends Ethel, Po-Yuk and Charles Okoye."

"For heaven's sake!" she exclaims. "Those aren't your friends."

"Yes they are!"

"No they're not. Your friends are called Steve and Chris, and they're both balding white middle aged men, just like you. You're just pretending to have a diverse range of friends so that it looks good to all the Virtue Signallers on Twitter."

You give a sardonic laugh. What does she know? You're the writer. You're going to write the story the way you want it. The way it needs to be written

BARBARA PICKED UP TONY'S STORY. She took the pen from the bedside table and settled herself back to begin editing.

Tony always forgot about this. He could write what he liked, but sooner or later he'd give her the story to edit…

She couldn't help but smile to herself. It was time, she thought, for a little omniscient narration…

ACKNOWLEDGEMENTS

ERIC BROWN

I'D LIKE TO THANK EVERYONE who has ever lived, from the first ape who swung down from the trees, stood upright and took that very first step, to the last human left alive on planet Earth.

Without you all, this book would be impossible.

I'd like to thank my mother and father, of course, because without their co-operation and effort I wouldn't exist to write this book. I miss you more than you might imagine. I'd like to thank my brother and sister, Dave and Amanda, for giving me the confidence to put those first tentative words on paper all those years ago. I think of you often, and miss you both. I'd like to thank my best friend Eddie, for being there when it mattered. Your death, perhaps more than all the six billion others, pains me deeply.

THIS BOOK HAS BEEN A massive undertaking. It took me twenty years to research, and almost as long to write. *A History of the World* in ten one hundred thousand word volumes is no small feat. The project kept me sane; without it, I might have gone mad with loneliness and grief.

I'd like to thank the Krenkle from Groombridge III, naturally. Without their encouragement, I would never even have thought of writing the history of my planet.

After the plague hit, we survivors formed a tight-knit, comradely band. Little by little, one by one, we succumbed to the inevitable: illness, accident, and old age. For a year I was alone, without purpose, other than the day-to-day scavenging in order to keep myself alive. There were days when the effort seemed futile. What, after all, was I keeping myself alive *for* – other than to die in agony, alone, at some point in the future: death lay in ambush, but when?

And then ten years ago you, my saviours, arrived on Earth. I recall the day well. I had just mined the last can of beans from the crumbling remains of the local Waitrose, and was contemplating making another foray to the Aldi store over in Bradford, when I saw your silver ship descend.

Oh, how I craved humanoid company! As the dust settled, and the hatch in the flank of your ship slowly opened, I fantasized about tall, beautiful golden human-like beings – beautiful women, preferably, but after a year alone, beautiful men would have been acceptable.

And what emerged? Forgive me – though I know you'll understand – but imagine my disappointment when what looked like three huge crabs appeared and skittered down the ramp.

My initial despair, however, was overcome when you proved to be wise, compassionate, and companionable beings. And then you commissioned me to write the history of my planet.

So here it is, all one million words – for your delectation and edification!

A SMALL PART OF ME will miss my world, of course. But I could not contemplate living here, alone, until such time as death might take me. Much preferable the offer you made in return for the book – a home of my own amidst the teeming multitudes of the galaxy!

But first the ultimate book tour of the Krenkle Empire where, I have been assured, a hundred billion eager extraterrestrials, of all shapes and sizes and colours, await to greet the author of the history of a world no more.

Adieu, farewell earth's bliss!

MANIFESTO

TONY BALLANTYNE

(I read the following at the launch party for *Dream Paris*,
11th Sept 2015.)

~

IT'S A COMMON QUESTION ASKED of all authors: why did you
write this book?

So when I finished *Dream Paris*, just like when I finished all
my other books, I sat down and thought about what my
answer would be when asked that question.

It was only then that it occurred to me how odd this was.
I'd just spent 381 hours or 15 and a bit days (I timed myself,
see my website) writing a novel over the course of a year, and I
hadn't once stopped to think why.

WHY AM I DOING THIS? Why write at all?

THERE'S A VERY EASY ANSWER to this. That great writer about
writing, Sol Stein, said that a writer was someone who couldn't

not write. But perfect though that answer is, it doesn't actually answer the question. Why write at all?

I spent a lot of time over the summer, wondering just that. I spend a lot of my time writing, my family put up with it, they've rearranged their lives to a certain extent to let me spend my time sitting at keyboard.

Why do I write? I could say it's because I'm a story teller, but every human is a story teller. The first story we tell ourselves is the story of who we are. We make up the story of what sort of a person we are: happy or sad or popular or deserving or hard done by. We make up stories about other people, our friends and acquaintances, and our stories about them never match their stories of themselves. We put ourselves in their shoes so we can try and understand their motives and actions. This is what scientists call a theory of mind, some say this is the dawn of intelligence.

So I don't think it's enough to say that I'm a story teller, because everyone is.

I COULD POINT OUT THAT like many people in this room I'm a professional story teller, what's called a teacher, and have been since I taught fencing on a children's camp in America and discovered to my surprise that I enjoyed it. All teaching is storytelling, teaching is taking the real world in all its splendid, unknowable complexity and reducing it to a story that a child can understand. Not only understand, but believe. And any teacher will tell you that the student doesn't always believe what you're saying.

So I'm a teacher and a writer. I don't know which of those things come first, I know that they're both linked. Incidentally, my wife often points out that those are two things nearly everyone thinks they can do until they try it...

Now, I don't know if the above explains why I'm a writer. I know it leaves me thinking who wouldn't want to be a writer?

But that still doesn't explain why I write what I write.

There's a certain cachet in being a writer, and whilst I'm delighted with this, it's a sign of our society that someone who has written an impenetrable 80,000 word novel about the pain of being middle class is generally held in higher esteem than someone who gives up all their free time to run a Scout Troop or a Brownie Pack.

It's also true that there is less cachet in writing SF. Indeed it's not uncommon for people to ask me if I ever intend to write a 'proper' book. And yes, that is as rude as it sounds.

Well, I believe that SF is the only truly original form of literature of the past 100 years. SF encompasses everything from the mainstream but adds its own unique sensibility. I believe that SF is read by people who appreciate the beauty in Euler's Identity just as readily as they appreciate the beauty in the St Matthew Passion, and if they don't understand either of those things then they don't scoff at them, they don't say they are boring they are pretentious, they set off to learn about them. SF recognises that there is as much beauty in maths and science as there is in the arts, and that all these things make humans what they are. In my opinion, to try and explore the human condition without acknowledging the cold equations is to fail as a writer.

I BELIEVE WHAT I JUST said to be true, and I could say that's why I'm an SF writer, but it's not.

THE TRUTH IS, I'M AN SF writer because when I write, I write SF. That's the way that I think. SF isn't about the robots and spaceships and rayguns—I rarely write about those things anyway—it's about the way you look at the world, it's the way that the stories are told. I can't write a story without extrapolating, without asking what if, without acknowledging the fact that there is a cold, impersonal but ultimately wonderful universe out there.

I WANT TO EXPLAIN THE world, I want to find wonder in the everyday. Ultimately, I think that the fact of the evolution of the horse is more wonderful than any unicorn and I can't pretend otherwise. That really would be selling out.

THIS IS WHY I WRITE.
    This why I write what I write.
    I can't help it, I have no choice.

MEETING MYSELF ON PLANET EARTH

ERIC BROWN

I WAS ENJOYING A QUIET lunchtime pint when the stranger approached me.

"I hope you don't mind my interrupting like this," he said, with a formality wholly in keeping with his appearance. He was a small, bald-headed man in a neat navy blue suit, with a totally nondescript face and a hesitant manner.

I smiled. "Not at all."

"The fact is, I have come rather a long way to meet you."

I stared at him. "You have?"

"A very long way, in a manner of speaking. You see, I admire your work."

It isn't every day that I'm approached by an admiring reader. In fact, it isn't every year... The truth be told: it's never happened in all the years I've been writing.

"Why... Thank you. That's very kind."

"Not at all. I appreciate how hard it is to write, and to keep on writing, year after year, with no recognition in the early years..."

And, I thought, scant recognition in the latter years.

But he went on, "And no recognition in the latter years." He smiled.

I sat up. Coincidence, surely?

"And the constant disappointments. The hope, forever dashed. The film offers that never come off. The publishers who don't pay on time, or who go out of business before publishing your work…"

He sounded like that part of my brain in constant dialogue with the rational part which says, 'Pack up and get a proper job.'

"You sound as if you're a writer yourself."

He smiled. "In a way, I suppose, you could say that I am."

"Ah… can I get you a drink?"

"That would be very kind," he said. "Perhaps a half of mild."

His choice was entirely in keeping. I ordered. "You mentioned you'd come a long way…"

"On a very important errand," he added.

"Quite." It would be just my luck if my first fan for a decade turned out to be a lunatic. "An important errand?"

"You see," he went on, "I have a favour to ask you."

Here it comes, I thought: he wants me to read his latest magnum opus.

"And that is?"

He hesitated, took a minuscule sip of mild, and smiled at me. "Perhaps, first, I had better explain my origins?"

I nodded, quite at a loss.

"You see, I come from the planet Earth…"

"Planet Earth?" I said.

"I can see that I am confusing you."

"Well," I allowed, "just a little."

"I'll explain: I come from Earth number three thousand and forty-five."

I repeated the figure and gestured around me. "And this Earth is?"

"Earth number three thousand and forty-six."

"Of course," I said.

The mild-mannered little man was, most assuredly, a lunatic.

He said, "My Earth is very, very different to this one – but still Earth," he hurried to assure me. "The inhabitants, for one thing…"

I peered at him. "You don't look too different," I said.

That meek smile again. "Oh, but I am wearing a human suit," he said.

I decided to play along with him. "A human suit… Well, it looks very authentic, I must say, Mr…?"

"Ah… Now that's where this might become even more confusing for you."

Might become? I thought.

"Try me."

He took a deep breath and said, "I am you, Mr Brown."

"I see. You're me. Well, you don't look very much like me, I must say. Sorry!" I said, slapping my forehead. "I forget, you're wearing a human suit. No doubt under the suit, you're the spitting image of me?"

He took a sip of beer. "Not at all," he said. "Under this suit I resemble an octopus."

I was beginning to enjoy this. "An octopus?"

"An octopus."

"And yet you claim to be me?"

"Indubitably. I am you. You see, on all the many worlds of the Polyverse, you – and everyone else on Earth – is duplicated in essence."

"Ah," I said. "In essence – but not in physical fact?"

"Quite. You see, each of us share the same...we share the same *quiddity*, if you like. The same identifying cerebral signature, all the way down the line of all the many millions of planet Earths."

I was beginning to find this fascinating; beginning, even, to think that there might be a story here.

"Is that so? But if I might ask... what exactly are you doing here? You said you'd come expressly to see me?"

"That is so. On my world, as you are here, I am a writer – though concomitant with the many differences between our worlds, you probably wouldn't recognise my vocation as that of a writer. But all that to the side. What matters is why I am here."

"Quite."

"You see, on my planet Earth, we have discovered the Truth."

"The Truth?"

"Exactly so. The Truth of the Polyverse."

"And this Truth is…"

He smiled, sipped his mild, then said, "The truth is that transformation from the physical form, *transcendence*, if you like, is not achieved through one's death, but is attained when one is able to communicate the fact of the Polyverse to the next 'you' in line along the string of Earths. Through the knowledge thus shared, one attains a kind of critical mass, and ceases to exist in the physical realm – one ascends to the realm of the non-corporeal – Nirvana, if you like."

"I see," I said, mulling over this gibberish. "But that begs the question: why, since you have done just that – communicated to me the fact of the Polyverse – are you still here, in the realm of the physical?"

"Aha!" he said as if catching me out. "The effect takes place after a short duration." He glanced at his watch. "In precisely," he continued, "two minutes. Now I shall walk through that door over there–" he indicated the door to the men's lavatory "–and when two minutes have elapsed I shall be no more." He looked around. "I would do it here, in front of you, but my sudden disappearance might cause consternation amongst the other customers."

I peered at him. "And you expect me to believe this?"

He smiled. "There are no windows in the men's lavatory, Mr Brown, and only one door…" He stood. "If you follow me after a few seconds, then you will find the room empty – so proving the veracity of my story."

He moved towards the toilet door.

"One thing!" I said. "How did you manage to transport yourself to this Earth?"

He paused, smiling back at me. "I am delighted you asked me that, Mr Brown. You see, the very act of writing down what I have told you in story form opens a temporal-spatial interstice in the Polyverse and allows you access to the next Earth in line. It is now your duty to write this story and proceed to the next Earth in line, where you will locate yourself and recount the Truth."

I pointed at him, convinced I'd found the flaw in his tale. "But how did you come by the human suit?" I asked. "And what if I find myself on an Earth where the people are wholly different in form from myself?"

He laughed at this. "But Mr Brown! You are a fiction writer! You merely use the power of your imagination and *think* yourself into the appropriate guise. And now," he went on, with a last look at his watch, "I must be going."

And so saying he turned on his heel, hurried across the room and slipped into the men's lavatory.

I counted ten seconds, twenty. After thirty seconds I left my table and approached the toilet door.

I was cautious, of course... What if the man were dangerous, and this was no more than a ruse to lure me into the toilets and accost me?

I pushed open the door and stepped inside. I peered around. The small, tiled room was empty.

I tried the cubicles, one by one – sure that I would find him hiding in one of them, grinning at my credulity.

I pushed open the door of the last cubicle and stared inside. My *alter ego* was not there.

TEN MINUTES LATER, HAVING ARRIVED home, I powered up my PC with trembling hands.

Having always believed in the transcendent power of the word...

...I opened a new file and began writing.

ERIC BROWN was born in 1960 and began writing in 1975 while living in Melbourne, Australia. He was the author of over fifty books in the science fiction and crime genres, and his work was translated into eighteen languages. He disappeared mysteriously from his home in Cockburnspath, Berwickshire, on the 24th of April 2016.

ACKNOWLEDGEMENTS

"The Robot and the Octopus" first appeared in *Nemonymous* 5, August 2005.

"The Cleverest Man in the World" first appeared in *Nature* 468, November 2010.

"Rondo Code" first appeared in *Nature* 498, June 2013.

"Takeaway" first appeared in *Nature* 458, April 2009.

"If Only…" first appeared in *Nature* 489, September 2012.

"Why are Rocks?" first appeared in *The Hub* 40, 2008.

"The Scooped Out Man" first appeared in *Daily Science Fiction*, June 14th 2016.

"Another (almost) True Story" first appeared in *Daily Science Fiction*, August 1st 2016.

"With this Bread", "Dear Burglar", "The Stars are Falling", "An (almost) True Story", "Plenty More Fish in the Sea", "Balance Sheet Clean", "Compatibility", "Future Tense", "Tony Ballantyne and Mr Brown", "Brought to Earth", "What Goes Around", "Would You Believe It", and "Manifesto" are original to the collection.

Tony Ballantyne would like to thank the following editors in whose magazines, websites and anthologies these stories first appeared: Lee Harris, D.F. Lewis, Henry Gee, Michele-Lee Barasso and Jonathan Laden.

~

"Differences" first appeared in *Albedo One*, December 2011.

"Diamond Doubles" first appeared in *Daily Science Fiction*, 16th July 2013.

"State Secret" first appeared in *Postscripts* 15, Summer 2008.

"Terortory" first appeared in *Fusing Horizons* 5, 2006.

"Aesthetic Appreciation On Asperex" first appeared in *The Hub* 144, 2012.

"Fixation Morbidity" first appeared in *Daily Science Fiction*, 3rd November, 2015.

"Reduction ad Absurdum" first appeared in *Pennyshorts.com*, May 2015.

"The Alien Tithe" first appeared in *Daily Science Fiction*, 6th March 2014.

"Visiting Planet Earth" first appeared *Daily Science Fiction*, 28th January 2012.

"Dead Reckoning" first appeared *Pennyshorts.com*, June 2015.

"In the Recovery Room" first appeared *Nature* 462, December 2009.

"Soul" first appeared in *Now We Are 5*, Summer 2011.

"The Hunt" first appeared *Daily Science Fiction*, 7th October 2016.

"Meeting Myself On Planet Earth" first appeared in *Moon Shots*, Spring 2014.

"Guns-U-Like", "Children of Earth", "Some Notes on Owning A Human Being…", "The Oth", "History of Planet

Earth", "Memorial", "Acknowledgements" are original to the collection.

Eric Brown would like to thank the following editors in whose magazines, websites and anthologies these stories first appeared: Robert Neilson, Michele-Lee Barasso, Jonathan Laden, Peter Crowther, Ian Whates, Lee Harris, Catherine Horlick, Henry Gee and Gary Fry.

TONY BALLANTYNE is the author of the Penrose and Recursion series of novels as well as many acclaimed short stories that have appeared in magazines and anthologies around the world. He has been nominated for the BSFA and Philip K Dick awards. *Dream Paris*, the follow up to the critically acclaimed *Dream London*, was published in September 2015. He is currently getting in touch with his SF roots by writing a Space Opera. Due to popular demand, he has also recently begun working on a series of short stories set in the Recursion universe. His website can be found at: http://tonyballantyne.com

ERIC BROWN has won the British Science Fiction Award twice for his short stories, and his novel *Helix Wars* was shortlisted for the 2012 Philip K Dick award. He has published over one hundred and forty short stories and sixty books, and his latest include the crime novel *Murder at the Loch*, and the SF novel *Jani and the Great Pursuit*. He writes a monthly science fiction review column for the *Guardian* newspaper and lives in Cockburnspath, Scotland. His website can be found at: http://ericbrown.co.uk

Printed in Great Britain
by Amazon